THE NANTUCKET INN

PAMELA M. KELLEY

PIPING PLOVER PRESS

INTRODUCTION

Lisa Hodges needs to make a decision fast. Thanks to her dead husband's gambling addiction, their savings is almost gone. In her early fifties with a large, waterfront home on Nantucket to support, Lisa hasn't worked in over thirty years, has no in-demand skills and is virtually unemployable.

Her only options are to sell the house and move off-island, or, she could use her cooking and entertaining skills and turn her home into a bed and breakfast. She desperately needs it to succeed because she has four grown children with problems of their own and wants to stay close to them.

Her oldest daughter, Kate, has a fabulous career in Boston--working as a writer for a popular fashion magazine and engaged to a dangerously handsome, photographer, who none of them have met.

Kate's twin, local artist, Kristen, has been reasonably content with her on-again off-again relationship with an older, separated businessman.

Her son, Chase, runs his own construction business and is carefree, happily dating here and there but nothing serious.

Youngest daughter, Abby, is happily married to her high school sweetheart, and they've been trying to have a baby. But it hasn't happened yet, and Abby wonders if it's a sign that maybe their marriage isn't as perfect as everyone thinks.

Come visit Nantucket and see how Lisa's new bed and breakfast has an impact on almost everyone in her family. It's the first book in a new series that will follow the Hodges family, friends, and visitors to Nantucket's Beach Plum Cove Inn.

CHAPTER 1

The money was running out. Lisa Hodges sighed as she sat at her kitchen island and looked over the month-to-date transactions in her checking account. How did it disappear so quickly? She couldn't remember the last time she'd bought herself new clothes, and she'd cut way back on going out to dinner with friends. But living on Nantucket was expensive, especially now that her husband Brian was gone—food, cable, insurance, it all added up too fast.

They'd been married for just over thirty-three years when Brian learned he had stage four colon cancer. Six months later, he was gone. That was almost a year and a half ago and when she'd finally been able to push aside her grief long enough to look at the bills, she'd been shocked at the state of their bank account.

Brian had always handled all the financial matters in their relationship. He earned the money, managed the banking accounts and paid the bills. She had access to their main checking account of course and knew there was always plenty of money in it to pay their day-to-day expenses. She also knew they had a healthy savings account that Brian regularly contributed to.

They'd always lived a comfortable lifestyle. Not extravagant, but there was always money for one or two vacations a year, college for the kids and dinners out a few times a month. And she'd assumed there was still a life insurance policy. She knew that at one time, there were million dollar policies on both of them. Brian earned his living as a financial planner and she'd always deferred to whatever he suggested as she'd never been good with numbers.

Lisa had been an English major in college and an elementary school teacher until she had the twins and then Brian pointed out that the math didn't add up for her to go back to work. They would pay as much in day care for Kate and Kristen as she'd earn teaching. So, the decision was made for her to stay home with their children. And she'd loved doing it. In the next few years, they had two more children, Abby and Chase.

Brian's only vice was that he was a bit of a gambler. He'd loved to go off-island with his buddies to visit the Foxwoods and Mohegan Sun casinos. And he and his friends always had poker nights the first Saturday of every month. She'd always assumed they played for small amounts and that it was all in good fun. It wasn't until Brian was gone and she dug more deeply into their finances that she discovered he actually had a serious gambling addiction.

Brian had stopped paying the premiums on their life insurance policies several years ago and the balance in their savings and retirement account was shockingly low. The retirement account was gone. There was nothing there at all. He'd withdrawn everything that was in their 401k, paid the penalties and used the money to settle debts that she'd never even known about.

There was money in their savings account still, but Lisa knew she'd have to cut way back on her normal spending habits to make the money stretch. By her calculations, if she did that, she might be able to make it stretch for almost two years, if she was lucky.

She wasn't too worried at the time though, as she figured she'd be able to get a job and the savings could be her safety cushion. But, she quickly found out that the market for fifty-something women with no recent work experience was nonexistent. And Nantucket was a small town, with limited opportunities.

She could possibly get a job as a cashier in one of the shops, but those paid minimum wage, which wouldn't go far. Restaurant work paid better. She knew that servers could do very well on tips, but she'd never worked in a restaurant and everyone wanted experience. It was almost time for her to make a big decision, one that she'd been putting off for as long as possible.

She sighed as she closed her laptop, stood up and peeked in the oven. The artichoke and spinach casserole was just beginning to bubble. In a few more minutes, the cheese topping would be golden brown and it would be done. Her two best friends, Paige and Susan, should be along any minute. They'd suggested going out to dinner, but she'd talked them into having appetizers at her house instead before they went downtown for the festive Nantucket Christmas Stroll.

It was always held the first weekend in December, and they looked forward to it every year. She'd been living on the island for over thirty years now and the stroll had been around even longer than that. It had started as a way for local shops to drum up a bit of business in the off-season and to prevent the locals from doing all their shopping off-island. It always felt like the official kickoff to the Christmas season.

Lisa stepped outside to check her Christmas decorations before her friends arrived. She'd just decorated the house earlier that day. She took a deep breath as she surveyed the house. Nantucket sound was just a few hundred yards away, and she could hear the waves as they crashed on the beach, a sound that she always found soothing. The air was cool and crisp, and she could smell a whiff of smoke coming from the fireplace of the house next door. She breathed in deeply as a gust of salty air blew her shoulder length hair back. She heard footsteps behind her and turned to see Paige and Sue coming down the walk.

"The house looks gorgeous! Where did you find that blue wreath? I love it!" Paige exclaimed.

"Do you really like it? I made it this morning." She'd walked along the beach and collected scallop shells and sea glass and used fine wire to wrap it around several pieces of driftwood that she'd glued into a circle and spray painted a pale blue. A snowy white bow at the top was the final touch. It had been a fun project, and she'd been pleased by how well it had turned out.

"It looks like you bought it at a fancy boutique," Sue said. "I brought my baked scallops," she added as Lisa opened the front door and they followed her inside. Paige was holding a platter and set it on the kitchen island and removed the tin foil cover. A selection of cheeses and sliced salami surrounded a small bowl of spiced nuts. She reached into her tote bag and pulled out a bottle of red wine.

"Peter said this one is supposed to be good. I haven't tried it yet." Peter Bradford was about their age and owned Bradford's Liquors, which was the only place to buy alcohol in Beach Plum Cove, the area of Nantucket where they all lived. Lisa found a wine opener and poured them each a glass. She set the bubbling spinach and arti-choke dip in the middle of the island and opened a box of crackers to serve with it.

They sat around the island, nibbling on everything as they sipped their wine. Sue's baked scallops were buttery, fresh and sweet, and Lisa was glad to see that her dip was a hit. When they were just about done, she brought up the subject that she'd been putting off as long as she could.

"If you were to use a realtor who would you go with? Missy Cunningham or Trevor Eldridge?"

Paige raised her eyebrows, "Who needs a realtor?"

"I might," Lisa said.

"I thought you said you'd never sell?" Sue looked confused. "You're not thinking of moving off-island?"

"I don't want to sell. But I may not have a choice. My money is running out, and even though the taxes on Nantucket are low, the real estate prices are high."

"But Brian was a financial planner. I thought you were all set for retirement," Paige looked both furious and worried at the same time.

Lisa sighed and then told them about the gambling debts and the retirement account and savings that had been drained.

"You didn't know about any of it?" Sue asked.

"I had no idea. Brian always handled that, and since it was what he did for work, I never thought to question him. I thought I would have been able to find a job by now. I really hate the thought of moving."

"Even if you sell, everything else on the island is expensive. You might have savings for a while, but you'll still need money to live," Sue said.

"I know. I've been trying to figure out a way to stay, but I am at the point now where I just don't think it's possible. At least there's no mortgage, so once I sell, I'll have a little time to decide what to do next. I could always rent for a while, maybe."

"Nantucket rentals are ridiculously expensive." Paige looked thoughtful as she added more wine to their glasses. "Your house is awfully big for one person. How many bedrooms do you have?"

"Six total. Five upstairs and the master on the first floor."

"Have you ever heard of Airbnb? You could make some money renting out the rooms."

"To strangers?" Sue sounded appalled at the idea of it. "That doesn't sound very safe."

"People do it all the time. It's the newest way to travel."

"I'm not sure how I feel about that," Lisa said.

"You're a great cook and you love to entertain and to decorate. You could turn the house into a bed and breakfast and still have plenty of room for yourself."

"A bed and breakfast, that is an interesting idea." Over the years, Lisa had thought more than once that it might be fun to own a bed and breakfast some day, to serve some of her home made favorites to guests. But dreaming about it was one thing, actually doing it was another.

"Would you actually consider it?" Sue sounded surprised.

"I don't think so. I love the idea, but I would imagine it would take a lot of money to get it up and running."

"I don't think it would. Your son is a builder. He could probably help you out. All you'd really need to do is close off most of the bottom floor so guests could only access the dining room and stairs to the second floor. And you'd still have your privacy." Paige made it sound so simple. Lisa didn't think that it would be, but she supposed it wouldn't hurt to at least act like she was considering the idea.

"I'll ask Chase to stop by one day this week and see what he thinks." She was pretty sure that he'd think they were all crazy.

"Have him over for dinner and make something delicious. Can't hurt…." Paige laughed.

"I'll do that. So, are you ladies ready to go strolling? I need to walk off this dip."

KATE HODGES RUSHED BACK INTO HER BEDROOM AND looked around until she saw the shoes she was looking for under Dylan's jeans. He'd left them in a crumpled heap on the floor, as usual. She slid her feet into them and glanced at the bed, where her fiancé lay sleeping. His dark hair fell over his forehead and he looked so sweet and peaceful. And so handsome, that he took her breath away. He yawned just as she turned to go and his sleepy voice stopped her.

"Is it that time already?"

"I'm going in early, it's not even eight yet."

Dylan stretched and grinned. "Kiss before you go?"

"I really have to run," Kate said as she walked over and kissed him lightly on the lips.

"My last shoot should end by six, want to meet me for dinner in the North End?" Dylan was a photographer and often did work for the magazine Kate worked for. That was how they'd met almost two years ago. He'd swept her off her feet, and she'd resisted as long as she could. Dylan was so charming and so good looking that it made her nervous. He was a flirt and girls were drawn to him. Kate didn't trust that his interest in her was real at first. But he won her over and six months later he'd proposed and she'd moved in with him.

They hadn't set a date yet as they were both very busy and for now it suited them to just live together. If Kate was being honest, she'd admit that she wasn't totally sure that what they had was a forever kind of love. Dylan was still a big flirt and sometimes it bothered her. He always laughed it off and told her she was being silly. And he was moody and distant at times. But whenever she'd question him about it he said it was just part of his creative process. And then he'd focus his attention on her fully and she'd feel foolish for doubting him.

"North End sounds great. I'll meet you at Al Dente at six." They almost always went to the same restaurant in Boston's Italian neighborhood. They'd had their first date there, and it was always so good. And then they'd stroll down Hanover street and share a cannoli at Modern Pastry. Kate's office near South Station was an easy walk there after work.

Their condo in the Charlestown Navy Yard was just a fifteen-minute ferry ride across the harbor to the Aquarium near South Station. Kate loved living in Charlestown and looking across the water at the Boston skyline. Although she still got homesick at times for Nantucket. As much as she would have loved to stay on the island with the rest of her family, Boston was where she needed to be for her career.

The office was quiet when she arrived. The only person there was Amanda, which was no surprise. Amanda was Boston Style's founder, and she was always in the office. She was an older woman, in her early sixties, divorced, and very stylish—she lived and breathed Boston Style. The magazine was a regional one with a focus on local fashion, food and politics. It was well respected and Lisa had felt very lucky to land a position there right out of college.

She'd started as an assistant, doing the things no one else wanted to do. But she'd done it all with a smile and an eagerness that had been rewarded. Her dream was always to write—anything from articles to columns and maybe someday, a book. She often did big investigative features which she'd won several awards for, and her mother bragged about them to all her friends.

Kate settled at her desk and quickly got lost in the project that had to be done by the end of the day. She finished a little before three and after emailing her feature to Amanda, she decided to reward herself with a vanilla chai latte. She was stiff from sitting and the walk would do her good.

Fifteen minutes later, she returned and was sipping her foamy drink as she came through the revolving front doors and almost walked into two laughing girls—Tasha, their Art Director, and Ellie, a drop-dead gorgeous blonde model they'd recently used for a fashion feature. Dylan had photographed her and had raved about her, saying that the light loved her.

But Ellie stopped smiling when she saw Kate. A cold look came over her face, and Kate took a step back in surprise. But Tasha didn't seem to notice.

"Hey, Kate! Tell Dylan when you see him that he really outdid himself. The last batch of photos he sent were amazing."

Ellie's expression changed again as she smiled and teasingly said, "Of course they were, I'm in them!" They both laughed and Kate smiled too. She must have imagined the frosty glare, or maybe Ellie had meant it for someone else as she was all smiles as the two of them walked off.

DYLAN WAS WAITING FOR HER AT THE RESTAURANT when she arrived a few minutes after six. Al Dente was just around the corner from Hanover street, where most of the restaurants and shops were. Kate always felt like she'd stepped into Italy whenever she went there. The food was always good, and the servers recognized them as regulars and always made them feel welcome. They had a delicious dinner as usual and were finishing the last of the bottle of chianti they'd ordered when Kate brought up going to Nantucket for Christmas.

"I talked to my mother earlier and everyone is coming over Friday for Christmas Eve. I thought we could stay until Monday and make a long weekend of it?" Dylan had only met her mother once, when she'd come to Boston and he'd never met any of her siblings, which they liked to tease her about. She understood somewhat though. It was a bit of a project getting to Nantucket. It wasn't like they could just drive over for dinner. It took some planning and Dylan traveled quite a bit for his work and so far, their schedules just hadn't worked to make it happen.

Dylan lifted his glass and swirled the wine around before taking a sip. He looked deep in thought and Kate started to feel her stomach tighten. She was counting on him to go to Nantucket for Christmas.

He took a long sip before saying, "I don't know if I can make that work, Kate. I have a shoot in California a few days before. I might need to stay longer. Plus my mother is in L.A. I can't go there without visiting her. You know how it is?"

She sighed. "I do. I just want you to meet the rest of my family. They tease me now that you don't exist."

He flashed her the smile that used to make her melt. "Why don't we go after the New Year? It won't be as busy, and we'll be able to see your family then?"

"We'll see. Maybe you'll finish up early and can visit your mom and still make it to Nantucket." Kate knew though, as she said it, that it wasn't going to happen.

"I'll try. No promises though." After paying the bill, Dylan smiled. "Did you save room for dessert? We could go to Modern?"

Kate wasn't the least bit hungry, but needed something to put her into a better mood. "Sure, let's get a cannoli."

THE LIGHT THAT HAD BEEN SO GLORIOUS ALL DAY WAS beginning to fade, and Kristen was too. She stood and stretched to relieve the muscles that had grown stiff from sitting in the same position all afternoon as the sunlight had poured in through the floor-to-ceiling windows. Her studio was a colorful mess, as always. Sketchpads were strewn about the room, canvases in varying stages of completion leaned against the walls, and magazines and books threatened to topple off her coffee table.

But she knew where everything was, and it worked for her. It was her happy place. And she was feeling good about her latest project. She was using a photograph she'd taken as inspiration for a watercolor, and it was almost done. When it was finished, she'd add it to the collection she was building for her next art show.

She glanced at the clock on the wall and began to feel stressed. Sean, her on-again boyfriend of sorts, was coming for dinner, and she still needed to shower and figure out what she was going to cook for him. When she'd invited him a few days ago, it had seemed like a good idea, but all she felt like doing now was taking a long, hot bath, and maybe pouring herself a glass of wine. But, she needed to get moving.

When she reached the kitchen, her phone rang, and the caller ID showed that it was Sean. He was probably running late, as usual. Ordinarily she'd be annoyed, but today, she welcomed the extra time.

"Hi Sean. What's up?"

"It's about tonight," he began.

"Are you running late? If so, no worries."

"No, it's not that. I'm sorry, but I'm going to have to reschedule. Andrea called to remind me that Julian has a big game tonight. If they win, they make the playoffs. I should be there."

"Oh, of course you should! We'll do it another time. Tell Julian I said good luck."

"I'll do that. Thanks for understanding. I'll call you tomorrow."

Kristen hung up the phone feeling both relieved and irritated at the same time. She was happy to have the night to herself, but hated picturing Sean sitting with his wife as they watched their son play basketball. It also annoyed her that they were still separated for over four years now and neither had filed for divorce yet. The few times she'd brought it up, Sean had just said that it was complicated and changed the subject.

Sean owned one of the most successful real estate offices on the island, and Kristen suspected that he wasn't ready to give up half of his financial holdings and Andrea wasn't ready to give up everything that went with being Mrs. Sean Prescott. Sean was well connected in town and had a membership at the most exclusive country club and their waterfront estate was massive. Andrea was still living there with Julian while Sean had moved into a smaller place, a condo on the pier, across from where the ferries docked.

Kristen was about to pour herself a glass of chardonnay and go sink into a hot bath when her cell phone rang again. This time it was Abby, her younger sister. Abby rarely called just to chat.

"Hey, Abby."

"Are you busy? I'm not interrupting anything, am I?" she sounded agitated.

"Of course not. I'm done for the day. Is everything okay?"

There was a long moment of silence before Abby spoke. "Yeah, it's just been a long day, and I'd love to meet for a drink and catch up unless you have other plans?"

"My plans just got canceled actually, so I'm all yours. Do you want to go out or come here? I have a bottle of wine I was about to open, and I could make us some pasta or something?"

"How about I bring our favorite pizza? I could pick it up and be over in about a half hour or so."

"Perfect."

Kristen took a quick shower and relaxed as the hot water soothed her tired muscles. She changed into her favorite yoga pants and a soft, long sleeved t-shirt and had just finished blow-drying her shoulder length, stick-straight brown hair when she heard footsteps outside. Abby had arrived.

She could smell the pizza as she reached the front door and opened it. Abby stepped in and handed her the box.

"Spinach, artichoke and feta?" Kirsten asked. "It smells amazing."

Abby grinned. "Of course."

"Great, I'll pour us some wine if you want to get the paper plates out of the cabinet."

She poured them two generous glasses of chardonnay and they each loaded two slices of pizza on their plates and went into the sunroom. Kristen's cottage was small, but cozy, and when she wasn't in her studio, she loved spending time in the sunroom. In the Summer months she kept the windows wide open, to let the fresh air in. She wasn't on the water, but even the most inland house on Nantucket still had crisp, ocean breezes.

In the cooler months, the room stayed warm because it faced the sun and she loved to curl up on the soft white sofa at the end of the day and read or watch a little TV. They settled on the sofa and put their wine and plates on the coffee table. The conversation was light and easy as they ate and sipped their wine. Abby hadn't mentioned anything out of the ordinary, but Kristen knew something was bothering her. After they finished eating, Kristen topped off her glass with a splash more wine, and noticed that Abby had barely touched hers, which was unusual. "So, why was today such a long day?"

Abby sighed. "I'm probably making too much of it. Jeff's really a great guy. I know that." Abby had married her high school sweetheart. She and Jeff had been dating since their sophomore year and got married a year after they both graduated from college. They were almost thirty now and as far as Kristen knew, they were happily married. Their only frustration was that they hadn't been able to get pregnant. Even after several attempts with IVF. And the process was much more difficult both physically and emotionally than Abby had expected. They'd all been surprised by that.

"What is it?"

"Well, it's just that he's never home. He works so much. More than ever before. He says it's because he needs to put in the time to grow the business, but it's almost like an addiction with him. He thinks about work, morning noon and night. And weekends too. I don't remember the last time we went away or even just went out to dinner. By the time Jeff gets home at night, he's so tired that he falls asleep on the sofa around seven."

"Have you talked to him about it? Asked him to cut back on his hours?"

Abby nodded. "Dozens of times. He always apologizes, cuts back for a week or two, then slips back into his usual habits. I've had it. And it's been a long time coming, but I finally decided that I can't live this way."

Kristen was shocked, as Abby and Jeff had always seemed like the most rock solid of couples. But, she also understood. If Abby wasn't happy she should do something about it.

"Are you considering divorce?"

"Yes, I have been thinking a lot about it recently. It's hard, but I finally made the decision to do it." She looked so devastated though that Kristen wrapped her younger sister in a hug and squeezed her tight for a moment. "I'm so sorry, honey." She tried to think of something positive that didn't sound like a cliche. But the best she could come up with was, "Well, maybe it's a blessing in a way that you had a hard time getting pregnant."

Abby looked as though she was on the verge of tears but laughed a little instead before saying, "Well, that's part of the reason why I wanted to come over here. I'd just made this decision, this big decision and then promptly threw up. At first, I thought it was nerves, or something I'd eaten, but then the thought occurred to me that it might be something else."

"You think you might be pregnant? But I thought the last round of IVF didn't work?"

"It didn't. And since we did two rounds back to back that failed, we were going to take the holidays off before trying again. I've been so stressed, and didn't think it was even a possibility without help, so I didn't realize that I was late."

"So, you are pregnant?"

"I don't know. I haven't checked it. I brought a pregnancy test with me. It's just so huge, if I am. Normally I'd check it with Jeff, but given what I've been considering…"

"Of course. I'm glad you waited to do it here. I'll support you, no matter what it says."

"Thank you." She took a deep breath. "I'm going to go check now." Abby grabbed her purse and went off to the bathroom while Kristen cleared their paper plates and put the leftover pizza in the refrigerator. When she was done, she went back to her sofa, took a sip of her wine and waited.

Finally, she heard the bathroom door open and Abby walked toward her, holding the pregnancy stick. Tears were streaming down her face and her eyes were red. She'd clearly spent several minutes crying after she read the results. Kristen got up and pulled her sister into a hug.

"I'm so sorry. It will happen for you, eventually. I know it will."

Abby hiccuped and sort of laughed a little as they sat back down on the sofa. She handed Kristen the pregnancy stick. It had two clear lines on it. She looked at her sister in confusion.

"You're pregnant?"

Abby smiled. "I am."

"But, that's great news! Jeff will be so excited. Maybe this is just what the two of you need."

But Abby shook her head sadly. "My baby doesn't need a father who is never there. I still want a divorce." Her voice broke a bit as she added, "or at least a separation."

CHAPTER 2

Abby left her sister's house and drove home, her emotions churning. She was excited to be pregnant, finally. It was just ironic that when they'd been trying so hard to make it happen, including with IVF and that didn't work, suddenly finding herself pregnant was a shock. She'd googled it though and learned that it wasn't all that unusual. Many couples failed to get pregnant and turned to adoption only to welcome a surprise baby of their own at some point. Doctors said it was because they were more relaxed and not anxiously trying so hard.

As excited as she was, Abby was still dreading the conversation that she knew she needed to have with Jeff. She hoped that they could get past this, and work it out, but they'd been down this road before several times. Each time, Jeff had promised to cut his hours back, and he had, but it never lasted for more than a week or two. And then he'd start going in earlier or staying later and either way, he'd inhale dinner and then fall asleep on the sofa around seven. Seven! She appreciated that he was a hard worker and knew that his family's business had more than doubled since he'd taken over, but at what cost?

And she didn't want him to agree just because of the baby. She didn't trust that it would last if he did. She needed him to see that he was killing their relationship even as his business thrived. He needed to find a way to delegate more and to get his life, their life back. But, she dreaded the conversation, and she knew she was feeling more emotional than usual because of the pregnancy hormones.

She stopped at the market on the way home and picked up a chicken, carrots and potatoes. She knew that Jeff would be sound asleep when she got home but she figured it wouldn't hurt to make his favorite dinner tomorrow.

So, the next evening, when Jeff walked through the door at a quarter to seven, the house smelled amazing from the chicken and vegetables that had been roasting in the oven. He stopped short and took a deep sniff.

"That smells fantastic!"

Abby smiled. "The chickens looked good at the market. Everything's ready if you are."

"Sure, you feel like a glass of wine? I'm pouring." He got two glasses out of a cupboard before Abby could speak.

"I'm just going to have water. My stomach is a little off." She already had a full glass of water that she'd been sipping on.

"Oh, okay." He put one of the glasses back and poured himself some merlot.

Abby made plates for both of them, and they ate at the kitchen table. Jeff talked excitedly about a new client he'd landed. She watched him as he spoke. He was so animated and earnest. She'd always loved how passionate he was about his work, before it took over everything. She loved how his eyes lit up as he spoke and how small laugh lines danced around the edges of his mouth. How his sandy brown hair fell over his forehead. It was thick and a little too long. He needed a cut, but she'd always liked it this way, on the long side. She sighed. She loved him dearly, but she just couldn't live like this anymore.

She knew she had a short window of time, maybe thirty minutes before she'd lose Jeff's attention. Before his eyes would grow heavy and he'd start to snore softly as he lay on the living room sofa. After he had a second helping of chicken, she cleared their plates and when he stood to go into the living room, she told him to sit back down.

"There's something I need to talk to you about." She knew that a certain tone had crept into her voice. It made him raise his eyebrows as he settled back into his seat.

"Is something wrong?" he asked as he took his last sip of wine.

She sat down too and folded her hands in front of her. "We need to talk. We've had this conversation before, and I can't do this anymore."

"What are you saying? Is it my hours? You want me to cut back again?"

Abby sighed. 'Not again. Not temporarily. I need a permanent change, Jeff. You leave before five most mornings, get home after six and you're dead to the world by seven. It's not fun for me or fair."

Jeff ran a hand through his hair and looked frustrated. "It won't be forever. But I need to be there."

"Why? You've got the company running better than ever. What time does Jason come in? When does he leave? What about your father and your uncles? None of them are putting in the hours you are. Are they?"

He was quiet for a moment and finally said, "Jason comes in when I do on most days."

"He doesn't stay as late though, does he?" Abby knew that he didn't.

"No, not usually."

"You're the one that's in charge. You should be able to find a way to delegate more so that you don't have to spend as much time there."

"I'll try. I'll see what I can do." He sounded frustrated and defensive, and Abby knew nothing was going to change.

"Jeff, seriously. I'm done, totally cooked. I can't go on like this. I think we need some time apart. To see if you can find a way to work out a new schedule and stick to it. A week or two isn't what I have in mind. I need a permanent change or we can just end this."

Jeff's jaw dropped. "You're serious?"

"Yes. I can move out, or you can." Abby knew she could stay with Kristen if she needed to.

Jeff was wide awake now and alternated between angry and panicked at what was happening. "You don't have to leave. We can work this out."

"I really think one of us has to leave for a while. We need a break. I'm hoping it will be a temporary one. If you really change your schedule and keep to it for longer than a month, we can revisit moving back in. I can go to Kristen's if you want me to leave."

"I can't believe you're doing this." He stood up and paced, and she could tell his mind was racing, processing what she'd said. He stopped finally. A decision reached. "I don't want you to leave. I'll go to Jason's." His voice broke a little and her heart did too when he asked, "Can I still see you?"

"Of course." She tried to smiled. "Maybe we'll go on a real date night."

Jeff didn't look at all happy about the situation. "All right. I'll pack a bag and head to Jason's. I guess I'll call you in a day or two?"

"So, what's this mysterious project that you want my help with? Are you serious about making your walk-in closet bigger? You've been talking about doing that for years." Chase teased Lisa as he leaned against the kitchen island. She'd invited him over for dinner and to ask his advice. She'd always thought of Chase as her golden child, her beautiful boy. His hair was the color of sunshine, and his eyes were a bright green with specks of gold. He was tall and lanky. He'd always been thin and able to eat everything without putting on weight. His eyes fell on the tray of stuffed shells that had just come out of the oven and were resting on a wire rack.

"And you made my favorite meal. I haven't had the shells in ages."

Lisa smiled. "I did. I like them too and as you said, I

haven't made them in a while. Let's sit down and eat, and I'll tell you what I'm thinking about. It's not a bigger closet." She set a bowl of salad in the middle of the kitchen table next to a loaf of crusty Italian bread and then dished out plates of pasta for both of them.

"Beer for you? Or wine?" she asked.

"I'll grab a beer, thanks." Chase helped himself to one of the beers that Lisa kept in the fridge just for him or anyone else that came by that liked beer. She didn't drink it. She poured herself a small glass of merlot and they sat down to eat. Over dinner, she told him about the idea the girls had that was growing more appealing as she thought about it. She was curious to see what Chase would think, both as a builder and as her son.

"You want to turn this place into a bed and breakfast?" He was surprised at first, but as they talked, and she filled him in on everything, telling him for the first time about the true state of her financial situation, his eyes narrowed with concern and then lit up as he looked around the room, assessing the possibilities.

"I'm sorry that Dad left you in this situation. I had no idea about the gambling."

Lisa sighed. "None of us did."

Chase took his last bite, then stood up and walked around the first floor, before returning to the kitchen table, where Lisa was still finishing her shells. She looked up and was happy to see that he was smiling.

"You could totally do it. If it means that you get to stay here, I'm all for it."

Lisa stood too and felt a glimmer of excitement and a fluttering of nerves. She knew that Chase would be the easy one. Her other children might not take this news as well. And she still didn't know if she'd even be able to afford to make the improvements. There was very little money left, for anything.

"Will it be very expensive, do you think?" She chewed her bottom lip and waited for bad news.

"No, it won't be. All I need to do is add a few walls and doors to close off your living area so guests only have access to the second floor and dining room." He gave her a figure that was shockingly low.

"I don't want you to lose money on this, honey."

But Chase laughed. "I won't lose money. You'll only pay for the materials and we won't need much. I can't charge you for my time. I want to do this for you."

Lisa felt tears of gratitude well up and spill over as she pulled her son in for a hug.

"Thank you. I'm so glad you think this is a good idea. I thought it was crazy at first, but it's kind of growing on me."

"I think it's a great idea. There's not a lot of jobs on Nantucket that would be good for you."

"That's a nice way of putting it," Lisa laughed.

"Seriously though. You love to cook, and you're good at it. And this is Nantucket, people will be happy to pay a lot of money to stay here, especially right on the water."

"I hope so. Now I just have to break the news to the girls."

Chase grinned. "Good luck with that." They both knew that the girls might not be as initially excited about the idea. "It won't take me more than a weekend to do this. I can have it done before everyone comes for Christmas."

"So soon?" Lisa was nervous about Chase starting the work so quickly. It made everything real. But it also made the most sense.

"Okay, let's do it," she said.

CHAPTER 3

C hange was in the air. Everyone could feel it. Amanda had been in closed door early morning meetings almost every day for the past week. And there had been an unscheduled board meeting in the conference room the week before. All kinds of rumors were flying around, but the one that made the most sense was that Amanda might be selling Boston Style. And the question on everyone's mind was what that might mean for the magazine and their own jobs.

Because everyone was worried, they were also bonding together. The Tuesday before Christmas week-end, Tasha, the art director, invited Kate to join her and a few others in the office for drinks after work. That had only happened once before that Kate could remember. She didn't really hang out with people in the office much since her friend Ashley, another writer, left to move to New York. That was right around the time she met Dylan and started spending all her time with him.

They went to The Black Rose, an Irish Pub in Faneuil

Hall, the historic brick buildings that were full of shops and restaurants. Tasha found them an empty table, and they ordered a round of drinks, Guinness beers for everyone except Kate who went with a glass of Cabernet. When the drinks arrived, Tasha raised her glass, "To hoping we all get to keep our jobs!"

"You don't think they'd actually lay people off right before Christmas?" Andi, a junior designer, looked horrified.

"They might. Lots of companies do. It helps them look more profitable before the New Year starts, or something like that," Tasha said.

"I can't imagine that Amanda would do that, not before Christmas. Though I couldn't imagine she'd ever sell either," Kate said.

"You'll probably be safe. You've been here forever, and you're her top writer," Tasha said.

Kate was thinking the same thing, but it seemed insensitive to say so. "I don't know about that. Hopefully no one will be cut and maybe there's something else going on, and the magazine isn't being sold. Maybe she's looking to expand?"

But Tasha laughed at the idea. "I don't think many magazines are expanding. Our numbers haven't grown in the past five years. We're holding our own, barely. Look at all the newspapers and other magazines that have downsized. Everything is moving to digital."

They were quiet for a moment. It was the truth. The internet had changed the media world considerably in the past ten years. Kate felt a little guilty thinking about it because she was part of the problem—she never bought a print newspaper anymore. She read all her news online. Although she paid for subscriptions to the Boston Globe and New York Times, she knew that many people only read the free content and revenues were continually decreasing with all media companies.

"On a different note, what's everyone doing for Christmas? Kate, is Dylan going with you to Nantucket?"

"No. He has a shoot in California and will be spending time with his mother in L.A."

"I didn't realize he had family out there. That's too bad."

"We're hoping to get to Nantucket maybe for New Year's Eve."

"Oh, that would be fun."

THEY HAD A SECOND ROUND OF DRINKS AND IT WAS A little before seven by the time Kate arrived home. She was surprised to see that Dylan wasn't home yet either. They usually talked or texted at least once during the day. She checked her phone to see if she'd missed a call and saw that she had a text message from him.

"Working late tonight, don't wait for me for dinner. I'll see you later."

She tried to remember what he'd said he was working on that would keep him so late. But it wasn't unusual for Dylan to work long hours. He was a perfectionist with his work and would keep going until the light was just right and he got the perfect shot, the one that matched his vision.

She wasn't starving and didn't feel like cooking much of anything so she microwaved a potato, threw some butter and Sriracha sauce on it, and called it dinner. She climbed into her pajamas after eating and curled up on the sofa to read for a while and watch a little HGTV. She was obsessed with the home renovation shows and how sometimes the simplest things, like a fresh coat of paint or a new floor, could make something look so much nicer.

Kate watched the news for a while at eleven and finally gave up on waiting for Dylan to come home and went to bed. She was just drifting off to sleep when she heard the front door open. Dylan came into the room, saw that the lights were off and that she was in bed. He quietly undressed and joined her.

"You're awfully late," she said softly.

"Yeah, it was a long day. I thought you were sleeping." He leaned over and gave her a quick kiss. She tasted alcohol on his breath, whiskey.

"I almost was asleep. Did you go out tonight?"

"Just for one. Tony was on tonight, and I stopped in for a quick drink to unwind. I figured you'd be asleep."

Kate wasn't sure whether to be annoyed or to appreciate his consideration not to disturb her.

"What were you working on that made it such a long day?"

"A catalog shoot for Murray's on Newbury Street. It's a huge project." Murray's was one of the most expensive boutique's on Newbury Street, Boston's equivalent of Rodeo Drive. "I was hoping to finish up today, but it looks like I need another day to do it right."

Kate yawned. "Okay. I have to be up early, so I'll see you in the morning."

DYLAN WAS DEAD TO THE WORLD WHEN KATE LEFT FOR work the next day. She told him she'd see him later that evening, and he just snored in reply. She figured he'd probably go in late and work late again. His schedule was more flexible than hers.

The mood in the office was still tense, but Kate relaxed a bit when she got a phone call around ten with incredibly good news. She'd been short listed for a major journalism award for an investigative feature she'd done earlier in the year. So, when Amanda emailed her at eleven and asked her to come to her office, she assumed it was to congratulate her as Amanda would have been notified as well.

She smiled as she tapped on Amanda's door, which was ajar.

"Come in and shut the door behind you."

Kate entered the room and shut the door which was a somewhat unusual request. Amanda usually kept her door open.

"Have a seat, Kate." Amanda indicated the leather chair across from her massive dark wood desk. It was set in the corner of a large room and faced out over Boston Harbor. Kate sat and waited.

Amanda smiled and tapped her hands nervously on her desk, finally steepling them and resting her chin on her hands as she looked at Amanda. "Congratulations on being short-listed. It's a well-deserved honor."

Kate relaxed a bit and smiled at the compliment. Amanda didn't hand them out often.

"But it makes this even more difficult. Kate, you're one of my best employees and longest term. I don't have a single complaint about your work. But, I've had to make some difficult decisions this week. You may have noticed we had a board meeting recently and there have been a lot of people in suits in and out this past week?"

Kate nodded and felt her stomach tighten.

"I never planned to do this, but I'm selling Boston Style. They made me an offer I couldn't refuse and well, I'm not getting any younger. I'll be staying on for a few years as publisher, but it won't be my company any longer. And the new owners are looking to cut costs. They are looking to cut most of the higher paid salaried writers and move to using freelancers. I'd love to still work with you, Kate, but on a consulting basis."

Kate's head was spinning. "Are you saying that I'm fired?"

Amanda flinched at the word. "Well, not exactly. Laid off is more accurate. You'll have a generous severance package of course. And I'd like to be in touch for future assignments, if you're interested? You'd be able to work from home, won't that be nice?" She tried to put a positive spin on a horrible situation and Kate felt suddenly nauseous.

"When… when do you want me to leave?"

Amanda thought for a moment. "Well, you just turned in your feature and a new column yesterday, so there's really nothing else pressing. You could finish up by lunch today and start your holidays early!" She smiled as if she was doing Kate a favor.

Kate slowly stood up and found her voice, although it was a bit shaky. "I hope you understand this is a bit of a shock? I really didn't see this coming. I thought, well, I thought I'd be safe. I guess that was silly?"

"I'm sorry, Kate. If it was up to me, this wouldn't happen." She stuck her hand out and Kate shook it. She was feeling a mixture of anger and despair and shock. She also felt her eyes welling up and wanted to get out of Amanda's office before they spilled over and added to her humiliation.

"Goodbye, Amanda. Merry Christmas," she added softly.

She left Amanda's office and went straight to the restroom, took a deep breath, and dabbed at her eyes. When she felt somewhat composed, she went to her desk and pretended that nothing was wrong. She spent the morning going through her emails and tying up loose ends, returning messages and setting up an auto-responder that simply said she was no longer with Boston Style and to follow up with Amanda.

When noon rolled around, and the office began to clear out for lunch, Kate grabbed her few personal items in her office, pictures of her and Dylan, a desk calendar, her favorite pens, and put them all in her oversized tote bag. And then she left. She walked out of the office without saying goodbye to anyone. She especially avoided Tasha as she knew she'd break down in tears if she had to tell her or anyone what had happened. Especially after

Tasha had said just the night before that of anyone, Kate was likely to be safe. She'd believed it too. Which in retrospect was naïve of her. The higher paid people were often the ones who 'got whacked' as Tasha had said. The expression had made Kate laugh when she'd first heard it. But she wasn't laughing now.

All she wanted to do was to go home and crawl into bed. She didn't expect Dylan would be home until late again and she was grateful to have the place to herself. She didn't feel like talking to anyone. After a good nap and a hot shower, she'd call her mother and sisters and commiserate. And then she'd think about what to do next. At least she did have a little time and income, her severance package included three months of salary.

When Kate reached their apartment, a wave of exhaustion rolled over her, and she suddenly felt bone tired and ready to drop into bed. She also felt another wave of tears brewing. She was an emotional hot mess. She turned the key in the lock and stepped inside. And then stopped short as she heard a sound. She thought her ears were playing tricks on her, but then she heard it again, soft laughter.

And it was coming from their bedroom. Kate quietly dropped her bag on a kitchen chair and slowly moved across the room. The bedroom door was ajar and when she reached it, she heard the laugher again. And saw Ellie's long blonde hair tickling Dylan's naked chest as she sat straddled on top of him.

A sound escaped Kate's throat, some kind of strangled cry she didn't even realize she'd made. But Ellie heard it and turned to see Kate in the door. Dylan turned too and then pushed Ellie to the side and flew out of the bed and came rushing over to her. But instead of immediately apologizing, his first words were, "What are you doing here?"

"I live here!" Kate found her voice and screamed. "What is she doing here?" She pointed at Ellie, who was scrambling to pull her clothes on. A moment later, Ellie slid by them and disappeared out the front door. Kate looked back at Dylan who was raking his hand through his long tousled hair. She looked at the rumpled bed and the ripped condom package on the nightstand.

"How could you?" she said.

"It just happened. It didn't mean anything. I swear it."

"How long has this been going on?" Now Kate understood the cold look Ellie had given her. Kate was in the way. But not anymore. It was what she'd been afraid of all along.

"Not long. It's meaningless, these models. They just throw themselves at me. It doesn't mean anything."

"And you do nothing to encourage it? Right. Dylan, I'm done."

"What do you mean? And what are you doing home at this time? Is everything all right?" He put his hand on her shoulder, and she flinched and took a step back. His touch repulsed her now, and she knew that she'd never be able to trust him again. She slid her engagement ring off and handed to it him. But he wouldn't take it.

"Don't do this. I promise, it won't happen again."

"No, it won't." When he didn't take the ring, she set it on the kitchen table and went to get her biggest suitcase. Two hours later, everything she'd brought to Dylan's was packed in either her suitcase or several large boxes. She had the place to herself as Dylan had finally realized she was serious when she asked him to please leave for a few hours to let her get her stuff together in peace.

As soon as he left, she called her mother, who answered on the first ring.

"Hi honey! Is everything all right?" Kate rarely called her mother during working hours.

"I've been better." She told her briefly about losing her job and that she and Dylan had broken up, but she didn't go into the details on what she'd walked into. That was a conversation for another time, over wine, with her mother and sisters.

"Just come here, honey. Stay as long as you like. If you hurry, you can catch the five o'clock fast ferry."

There was no way Kate was going to miss that boat.

"Love you, mom. See you soon."

KATE DROPPED HER THREE BOXES OF STUFF AT THE local UPS store which was just a few blocks away. She had everything shipped to her mother's house and then only had to bring her large suitcase and carryon with her. She decided against taking the ferry which would have meant a bus ride to Hyannis first and instead splurged on an Uber to Logan airport and a direct flight to Nantucket.

She'd thought she was handling everything well, but once they were airborne and she looked out the window and saw the tangled mess that was Boston's twisting streets below, she felt the tears come again, fast and furious. She managed to find a half-used tissue in her coat pocket to staunch the flow of tears and kept her face turned to the window, so the other eight passengers on the tiny plane wouldn't notice.

Fortunately, the flight was a quick one, and they were soon landing at Nantucket airport. Kate had to fight tears back again when she stepped off the plane and smelled the fresh island air. Everything seemed to be triggering her emotions. She'd only taken a few steps when she heard a vaguely familiar voice right behind her.

"Kate Hodges, is that you?"

She turned and was surprised to see Jack Trattel.

"Jack! It's been a long time. Were we on the same plane?" She hadn't taken any notice of the other passengers.

"It seems that we were. I didn't notice until just now though. I was sitting a few rows behind you. It's good to see you. Are you home for the holidays?"

Kate hesitated and then smiled. "Yes, for a long Christmas vacation. Same for you?"

"Oh, I live year round on the island. I was just visiting my father at Mass General. He had heart surgery."

"I hope he's alright?" Kate remembered Jack's father as a big, strong man. A scallop fisherman.

"He will be. He's in one of the best hospitals in the country. They did his surgery robotically, so instead of several months to recuperate, he'll be up and around in three weeks."

"That's good news. Are you still working with him?" Kate remembered that Jack worked with his father during their high school years. She hadn't run into Jack much after that. It had been years since she'd seen him.

"I am. He retired a few years ago actually and I've grown the business a bit since then." He spoke modestly, but Kate remembered that Jack had always done well in school, and she had a feeling his business was doing quite well. She was happy for him.

"That's great. You're lucky being able to stay here year round."

"You live in Boston though, if I remember? That must be fun too." Jack smiled as they walked into the baggage area and waited for their luggage to be brought in.

"It can be. But there's no place like home," she said wistfully. When she'd graduated from Boston College, it had been a given that she'd search for work in the Boston area as that's where all the big newspapers and magazines were. She'd worked at the Nantucket paper one summer, but there were rarely any full-time openings as no one ever left.

"Jack!" They both turned to see a pretty blonde woman walking toward them. She looked familiar too as she wrapped her arms around Jack's neck and gave him a kiss. She had stick-straight, shoulder-length, blonde hair, blue eyes, and was a size two maybe even a zero. Cissie Anderson looked like she'd hardly aged since high school. She'd been a year behind Kate and Jack.

"Cissie, you remember Kate Hodges? She was on the plane with me, coming home for the holidays."

Cissie smiled, "Your sister is the artist, right? I see her painting down by the pier sometimes."

"Yes, that's Kristen. She always liked that spot."

Kate spotted her bags and grabbed the carryon first. She turned to get the big suitcase, but Jack had already lifted it down for her.

"It was great to see you, Kate. Say hello to your family. And Merry Christmas!"

Kate smiled as Jack and Cissie walked off. Cissie was chattering as Jack looked amused. It had been nice to see familiar faces.

"Kate!" Her mother had arrived and pulled her in for a tight hug. Kate felt the tears threaten to come again, but fought them back.

"I'm sorry I wasn't here when you landed, honey. I got stuck in traffic, behind a school bus."

Kate laughed. "No problem, we just got here, and I was chatting with Jack Trattel, you remember him?"

"Of course. Didn't his father just have a heart attack? I hope he's ok?"

"Jack was just visiting him in Boston, at MGH. He said his surgery went well."

"Oh, that's good. Well, let's get you home, shall we?"

KATE'S MOTHER CHATTED ALL THE WAY HOME, FILLING her in on all the island gossip, which meant Kate just had to listen and nod, which was perfect. She wasn't ready to talk about what happened with Dylan just yet. When they pulled into their driveway, she noticed that something was different.

"Did you paint the house?" It looked cleaner, fresher somehow.

"Just the trim. It was peeling in spots and that cleaned it right up."

"Well, it looks great. You made that wreath on the front door, I bet?"

Her mother smiled. "Yes. I'm particularly proud of that one. Everything came from our beach."

Kate got her luggage out of the car, and her mother grabbed her carryon. As they reached the front door, she said, "I made a few changes inside too." Her mother unlocked the door and stepped inside. Kate followed her in and stopped short.

"What is this?" They were standing in the front hall, with the dining room to their right, the stairs to the second floor in front of them and on their left, where the entrance to the living room used to be, there was now a wall and door.

"It's an experiment of sorts. Come in and have a cup of tea, and I'll fill you in. Oh, and everyone is coming for dinner tonight. They can't wait to see you, and except for Chase, they haven't seen these changes yet either."

AN HOUR LATER, LISA PULLED A TRAY OF HER children's favorite appetizer, sausage stuffed mushrooms, out of the oven. She'd also made the cheesy taco dip that Abby loved and had Kristen's favorite, chilled shrimp cocktail. Chase already approved of her plan, but she'd made his childhood favorite too, because she knew they all loved the tiny hot dogs wrapped in puff pastry.

She had beer and chardonnay in the fridge and an open bottle of cabernet on the counter. They should all be arriving any moment.

"I'm ready for a glass of red, what can I pour for you, mom?" Kate asked.

"I'll have red too."

Kate had taken the news relatively well. She was always the sensible one, her oldest child, even if it was just by a minute over her sister. Like Chase, she'd been shocked to learn the truth about the family finances. Lisa suspected that there was quite a bit more to Kate's story about her breakup with Dylan. But Lisa knew Kate was still dealing with losing her job too, and she didn't want to push her. She'd open up when she was ready. And Lisa was sorry that her daughter was hurting, but she wasn't sorry that the relationship had ended.

She'd met Dylan once and hadn't been impressed. She understood why Kate was drawn to him. He was the typical beautiful bad boy that was impossible to resist. Lisa had known someone like that once and she'd been tempted but had resisted. She'd somehow known even at a young age, that it would go nowhere good.

Lisa settled onto one of the chairs around the island and reached for a shrimp and dunked it into a bowl of cocktail sauce. Kate was perched on another chair and was dipping a chip into the taco dip. A moment later, they heard voices. Chase and Abby had arrived and Kristen was right behind them.

They walked into the kitchen and Chase immediately

came and gave Lisa a hug, then grinned and grabbed a handful of the hot dogs in pastry. "Thanks for making these." He looked around the island at all the appetizers and laughed. "You made all of our favorites!"

Abby and Kristen looked confused. "What is going on here?" Abby asked.

"Chase, you knew about this?" Kristen asked.

"I did it. At Mom's request of course."

"Did you know about this too?" Abby looked at Kate who had a mouthful of taco dip. She shook her head and then nodded, swallowed and finally spoke.

"I just found out today. Pull up a chair. Mom has a plan."

"What can I get you all to drink?" Lisa asked. "Chase there's beer in the fridge. Kristen there's red and white and Abby, I have your favorite chardonnay, Bread and Butter."

Chase grabbed a beer, while Kristen poured herself a glass of red and Abby sat and looked miserable.

"I'll just have a soda water, if you have any." Everyone looked at her in surprise and she added, "My stomach is a little off."

"I think I have a bottle of orange flavored seltzer, is that good?"

"It's fine, thanks." Lisa found the beverage and handed it to her youngest daughter. Once everyone settled with the drinks and had plates of food in front of them, Lisa filled them in. When she finished her story, there was a moment of silence, and then Chase spoke.

"I think it's a great way for Mom to earn money."

"But it's our house! Strangers will be staying in my

bedroom. I hate the idea," Abby pouted. Lisa was a little surprised at her reaction. She wasn't usually so emotional.

"I don't know how I feel about it either, to be honest. Is it even safe for you?" Kristen asked.

"It should be perfectly safe. That's why Chase put the walls up, so my living area is private from the rest of the house.

"I thought it was strange at first, too," Kate admitted. "But the more I think about it, the more I really like the idea. It seems perfect for Mom. She loves to cook and take care of people, and she has this huge house by the water that she's paying money to heat and not using all of it."

"Thanks, honey." Lisa looked around the table at all four of her children. "To be honest, I'm not entirely sure how I feel about it either. One minute I'm excited, the next I'm nervous. As you said, this is my house and strangers will be staying here. But, at the same time, it feels right and like a new adventure."

She grinned and added, "Besides, I'm too old and unskilled to do anything else on this island. My options are limited."

Kate stood and gave her a hug. "You are hardly old! But I do agree that your options are limited here. It's not just you. I'd love to stay here year round, but there are no newspaper or magazine jobs either. It's a beautiful place to live, but it's best if you're either rich or have some kind of business."

"And now Mom will have that business. People will pay crazy money to stay on Nantucket," Chase said.

"I can help you get ready too. Since I may be here for

a while," Kate said. The others all looked at her, and she took a deep breath and explained. "I just got laid off, and I broke up with Dylan. Double Whammy. So now I have no job and no place to live."

Kristen and Abby jumped up and hugged their sister and when they finished, Chase stepped in and did the same. Lisa loved that her children were all so close.

"That sucks that they laid you off right before Christmas," Kristen said.

"The bastards!" Chase said, and they all laughed.

"It is lousy of them," Lisa agreed.

"Amanda said it wasn't personal, just business. She said it was a difficult decision, but I don't really think that it was. She's always been all business."

"What happened with Dylan?" Abby asked.

"It doesn't matter what happened, just that it's over," Lisa said quickly. She sensed that Kate didn't want to talk about it. Kate shot her a grateful glance and then took a big sip of her wine.

"He cheated on me. I had just been laid off, came home to curl up and go to sleep, and he was in our bed with one of his models."

"Oh, no! Kate, I'm so sorry," Abby looked horrified. Lisa's heart went out to her daughter. What a truly horrific day she'd had. She put her arm around Kate's shoulders and gave her a squeeze. "I always thought you were too good for him," she said softly.

Kate's eyes misted over. "Thank you. To be honest, it was always in the back of my mind, something I'd worried might happen one day. He had a reputation, and he was too good-looking."

"Hey, now. Not all good-looking guys are cheaters!" Chase said and flexed his muscles. They all laughed. Chase had a way of lightening the mood.

"If you're serious, Kate. I really could use your help. I think I want to put a website up and I'm not really sure where to start," Lisa admitted.

Kate perked up. "Oh, I could totally help with that. You'll need some brochures too. I can write the copy and we can get it up on the web and maybe bring some brochures to distribute on the Cape. Lots of tourists decide to come to Nantucket after staying on the Cape."

"That's a great idea." Lisa turned to her youngest daughter, who'd been very quiet and had barely touched her seltzer water.

"How's your stomach honey? Are you sure you don't want a glass of wine?"

But Abby shook her head and sighed. "No, I'm actually not going to have any wine for a while. I'm pregnant and I told Jeff that I want a divorce."

Everyone stared at Abby in shock, except Kristen, Lisa noticed.

"Congratulations on the baby, honey! That's fantastic news. But are you sure about divorce? How does Jeff feel about all this? He must be over the moon about the baby."

Abby was silent for a moment and then said, "He doesn't know about the baby."

"You didn't tell him?" Even Kristen seemed shocked.

Abby shook her head. "I'm not telling him for three months. Until I know the baby is safe, that it's real. If we're going to work things out, I don't want it to be because of the baby."

"Do you want to stay here? You're welcome to." Lisa was overjoyed that Abby was finally pregnant, but she felt terrible that they were considering divorce. She'd always loved Jeff like a son. And she and Abby had been together forever it seemed.

"No, thank you. Jeff moved out yesterday. Besides, you need to rent my room out."

That stung. "Honey, I'm sure all my rooms won't rent out immediately. It is winter after all. The off-season."

"You might be surprised mom. It's not as busy, but people still come here," Chase said.

Lisa laughed. "Well, I hope you're right." She turned back to Abby. "Honey, we're here for you. Whatever you need. I really hope that you and Jeff can work things out."

"I do too."

AFTER EVERYONE WAS GONE AND KATE WAS IN BED, Lisa stayed up, reading in her bedroom and reflecting on how the evening had gone. Somewhat better than expected actually. She'd suspected that Abby would be the one most resistant to change, but she wondered if it was mostly just her being overly sensitive due to being pregnant.

Lisa felt a mix of joy and concern for her youngest daughter. She knew how badly she'd wanted to get pregnant, but to even contemplate divorce and being a single mother. It was such a big decision and would be a huge lifestyle change.

If what was wrong couldn't be fixed, then she'd fully support the divorce of course and try to help Abby as much as possible. She looked forward to babysitting and being a grandmother. But, she hoped that Abby and Jeff could get past this speed bump in their marriage. Every marriage had its ups and downs. Though as newlyweds, you never expect it will happen to you.

CHAPTER 4

The next morning, Lisa was up early as usual, and had just settled at the kitchen island with her morning coffee and a bowl of oatmeal when Kate bounced into the room full of energy. Lisa smiled when she saw her.

"Good morning. You're up early."

Kate went straight to the Keurig coffee maker and popped in a K-cup of dark roast coffee.

"I slept like a baby. There's nothing like being home, in my own bed. And it's so peaceful here. I left my curtains open and the morning sun woke me. It looks like it's going to be a beautiful day." When her coffee finished brewing, she added a splash of milk and joined Lisa at the island.

"What are your plans today?" Lisa asked her.

Kate laughed. "I have none. What are you doing? Can I help with anything?"

"I have to go downtown to do some grocery shopping.

I thought I'd poke around the shops too and see if there are any good bargains. I'm not looking to spend much, but I feel like I need to decorate the upstairs bedrooms a little more. Any suggestions?"

"That's a great idea. I'd love to help. And I know exactly what you need."

"You do?"

"New bedding. Good quality, all cotton white sheets, soft beachy colors for the bedspreads and a few pretty throw pillows. We can check any estate or yard sales to see if there's anything interesting to hang on the wall."

"Hmm. I was wondering if I needed to get new bedding."

"Definitely. And you don't have to spend much. We won't pay full price for anything."

Lisa laughed. "Nantucket prices are the worst." It was true, some of the shops downtown were ridiculously expensive. One of Lisa's favorite shops to browse sold nothing but cashmere sweaters and most were $800 and up.

"We'll be shopping for bargains and getting ideas. If we see things we like that we can't afford, we'll search for something similar online," Kate assured her.

THEY HEADED TO TOWN AN HOUR LATER AND SPENT THE morning mostly window shopping in dozens of stores. Their only purchases were five pretty, dried starfish at a yard sale. They got them for next to nothing as the woman having the sale was moving off island and was getting rid of everything.

"These will look perfect upstairs. You can hang them on the doors, right above the numbers. It will look awesome," Kate said.

Lisa hadn't thought that she'd need to put numbers on the doors, but it made sense, and she agreed that the starfish would give a pretty, welcoming look.

After they finished shopping, Kate insisted on paying for lunch at Black-Eyed Susan's, one of their favorite breakfast and lunch restaurants. After they ate, they went home, and Kate hopped on the internet. In minutes, she'd found bedding that was very similar to what they'd seen downtown, but it was on sale for a fraction of the cost. And the colors were so pretty too. They ordered sheets, and cozy looking bedspreads in soft sea shades, pale blues and greens. They found some pretty throw pillows too.

"There, that's done," Kate said, after she clicked the button to confirm their order. "What's next?"

Lisa laughed. "I'm not sure. I should make a list." She found a notebook and a pen, and she and Kate made a checklist of everything she needed to do before opening.

"Do you need any kind of permit? Or is this like an Airbnb?" Kate asked.

"Oh, I'm not sure. How does Airbnb work?" Lisa had heard of it, but never used it as she rarely went off-island.

"Airbnb is great actually. Dylan and I used it last spring when we went to Charleston for a long weekend. We found a great place in an old Southern home. The owner had divided the building into six units. It was just like a bed and breakfast but didn't have a sign. And it was much cheaper than a hotel."

"Hmm. Well, I don't want to be cheaper necessarily."

"No, I think on Nantucket, it might be better to go the opposite way and position your bed and breakfast as more high end. Though, you could still use Airbnb to fill in gaps when you aren't rented."

"Hmm, that's an interesting idea."

"Have you thought about a name?"

Lisa smiled. "I have actually. I was thinking of The Beach Plum Cove Inn."

Kate looked enthused. "Oh, that's perfect! And it tells visitors where you're located—that's always good for a business. And as far as I know, there are no other bed and breakfasts in Beach Plum Cove. They are mostly all downtown or out in 'Sconset."

"So, that's a good thing, right?" Lisa thought it should be, but she also worried a bit that maybe there was a reason that there were no competing businesses in the area.

Kate looked a bit concerned too. "It could be awesome, as long as there are no restrictions against it. Nantucket can be funny like that."

"I need to look into the process for getting a business license." Lisa knew that some new business licenses, such as restaurants or liquor stores needed to be approved by a board of selectmen. She had a feeling that a bed and breakfast might fall into that category and mentioned it to Kate.

"Well, if they say no, you could still Airbnb it, but it

wouldn't be as lucrative. You wouldn't be able to have a website or put a sign up advertising The Beach Plum Inn. How often does the board of selectmen meet?" Kate asked.

"The first Monday of every month. So, the next meeting will be right after the New Year."

"Oh, that's good. We should be ready to go by then. I'm sure they'll approve you," Kate was so confident. Lisa hoped that she was right.

KATE HAD TRIED HER BEST NOT TO THINK ABOUT anything since she'd been back on Nantucket. She didn't want to think about Dylan or the job that she'd loved that had been yanked away from her. She knew that she had to think about what she was going to do next eventually, but for now she just wanted to sink into the familiar comfort of home—to walk along the beach, listen to the waves crash on the shore and drink in the clean salt air.

She was enjoying spending time with her mother and helping her get ready for her new adventure. Kate had been skeptical at first, but the more she researched, the more excited she got about the idea. There was nothing else in the area, and it was one of the more desired spots on the island. Beach Plum Cove had the nicest beaches, and it was only a short drive or bike ride to downtown.

And she'd had fun working on a website for her mother. Kate's technical skills weren't strong, but there were so many programs now that made building a website fairly easy. She made a simple one with lots of white space and pictures of the beach and the front of the house with its white shutters and inviting wrap around farmer's porch.

Over glasses of wine one night, she and her mother discussed their ideas for how to present The Beach Plum Cove Inn and what they wanted potential visitors to know. They shared unique facts about the island and high-lighted different events that happened throughout the year such as the now famous film festival, wine events, Daffodil weekend, and the Christmas Stroll.

Kate suggested talking up how peaceful and relaxing Nantucket was in the off-season when you didn't have to fight the crowds. And Lisa came up with the idea to name all the rooms and to have a theme for each, based on the decor. Kate's favorite room, which had been her own, was the Piping Plover, named after the tiny birds with tooth-pick thin legs and cute, round bodies. They were endan-gered, and the beaches were often closed or access restricted when the birds were nesting.

The biggest room was the ACK room, named after the Nantucket airport and had several antique model planes and photos on the walls. It also had a leather arm chair and a bit more of a masculine feel.

Then there was the Figawi room, named after the world famous race that happened every Memorial Day weekend, when sleek expensive sailboats with full crews raced from Hyannis to Nantucket and back. Photos in this room were all boat related and there were also several wooden model boats that Kate's grandfather had painstakingly made and had cased in Plexiglass to protect them. He'd loved boating and always owned a boat and built models as a hobby.

Next was the Nantucket Red room, with white bedding, blue and white pinstriped wallpaper and cheery Nantucket Red curtains, the pinkish-red shade that was unique to Nantucket.

Lastly, there was the Daffodil room, which was a beautiful cozy room that was designed to make a woman feel pampered. The colors were soft shades of yellow and pale blue accented with white and there was a gorgeous painting of Daffodil weekend, with its array of yellow flowers and the famous parade of vintage vehicles and people enjoying their fancy tailgate picnics with champagne and filet mignon.

Her mother had wanted to hold off on renting out Kate's room, but Kate wouldn't hear of it.

"Don't be silly. If someone wants to rent it, do it. I can crash on the sofa or go bother Kristen or even Abby. She might like the company, actually." Both Kate and her mother were worried about Abby.

"We'll see. I'll rent the other rooms first. If anyone wants to rent them, that is. What if no one does?" She looked dismayed at the thought.

"Of course they will. We can run some Facebook ads too. I learned a little about that at the magazine. We can get really targeted with who we want to reach."

Her mother looked both intrigued and intimidated by the idea.

"That sounds lovely, but I wouldn't know where to begin with that."

"I can look into it for you. And if you sign on with

Airbnb, they get a small percentage but in return they send traffic your way."

"Okay. I still need to figure out pricing. Chase made some suggestions, but they seemed much too high to me."

Kate laughed. "Mom, Nantucket is ridiculously overpriced. If you don't price high, people will think there's something wrong. High pricing is part of the exclusivity factor."

"Hmm. I suppose you're right, but I don't want to price nice people out of coming either."

Her mother was so not a business person.

"Why don't you do some searching and see what some of the other bed and breakfasts are charging? The rates are going to vary quite a bit depending on location and time of the year, but you'll get an idea of what the going market rates are."

"Right. I'll do that. I looked initially and was encouraged by what seemed possible, but I'll be more thorough about it."

"And I'll go with you to the board of selectmen meeting. Hopefully that's just a formality," Kate said. Her mother had found out that an official bed and breakfast business would need to be approved by the board of selectmen. They were considering approval of another business that night too, a new restaurant that would be opening in Beach Plum Cove, which Kate was excited about.

From what she read in the local paper, it was pretty much a done deal as the new owner of the property was an experienced restaurateur and he was taking over a location that had been sitting empty for several years. It would be nice to have a good restaurant in their neighborhood again, and it would be a draw for the bed and breakfast too as it was within walking distance.

Kate was about to head over to Abby's for coffee when she noticed her phone lighting up with several text messages in a row. The first two were from Dylan, begging her to call him. He'd left voice messages too, apologizing profusely and asking her to give him another chance. She'd deleted the messages and had ignored the texts, but it was getting ridiculous. Ignoring him only seemed to make him more persistent. She sighed heavily and texted him back.

Dylan I can't go back. I'm sorry, but this is a deal breaker for me. It's over. Please stop calling and texting. She clicked send and then read the next text message, from Amanda.

Hope you're well. Merry Christmas! If you're interested, I have an intriguing feature I'd love to assign to you. Say the word and I'll email you all the details.

Kate's first reaction was irritation as she remembered how awful it had felt to be laid off.

But curiosity won out, and she typed back, *I might be interested. Tell me more.*

The text back came almost immediately. *Sent. Check your email.*

Kate checked her email and was surprisingly impressed. The assignment seemed tailor made for her. Amanda wanted her to do a feature on the coming year's Nantucket Film Festival, covering who would be there, how the event originated and interviews with some of the founders and presenters, which included some famous filmmakers.

Nantucket and Martha's Vineyard, the other island off the Cape, both attracted their share of celebrities that visited and owned properties. And the flat fee for the feature was more than generous. She didn't know how often Amanda might send freelance work like this her way, but if it was often enough or if she was able to generate other freelance assignments, maybe she'd be able to stay longer on Nantucket.

She quickly texted back to Amanda. *I'm in. Thanks for thinking of me. I'm actually here on Nantucket for a while.*

And the almost immediate reply back. *Great. I thought you might be.*

LISA WAS CAUGHT UP IN THE CHRISTMAS SPIRIT AND felt optimistic about the upcoming board of selectmen's meeting. She agreed with Kate that it just made sense that they'd be approved as well as the restaurant. On Christmas Eve, she held her traditional open house and all her children came, as well as her friends, Paige and Sue. The only person missing was Abby's husband Jeff, and it seemed strange that he wasn't there, but Lisa was hopeful that it was the only year he'd miss.

Abby seemed to be in good spirits, aside from the near constant morning sickness that often came with the first trimester. Lisa had it with all of her pregnancies but assured Abby that once she was into her fourth month, it was so much easier.

Kate had helped her to get ready and made a delicious light hummus from white beans, garlic, lemon and parsley. They served it with fresh-cut veggies and pita chips. Sue brought baked scallops wrapped in bacon and Paige brought several bottles of Prosecco, their traditional Christmas Eve bubbly wine. The star of the show was the fresh lobster casserole topped with crushed Ritz crackers and lots of butter. They also had shrimp cocktail and Chase brought a tenderloin that he'd grilled.

They ate and drank and the conversation centered on the plans for the bed and breakfast. Everyone was excited about it now. And though they didn't usually exchange gifts on Christmas Eve, after they ate, Chase went to the Christmas tree where they'd all dropped off their gifts earlier and picked up a large box with a bright red ribbon. He brought it over to Lisa and set it on an empty stool.

"Mom, this is for you, from all of us, and we're excited for you to open it tonight."

"Are you sure?" Everyone stared at her expectantly.

"Just open it." Chase grinned as she carefully tore off the wrapping paper. She had no idea what it was. And the bare cardboard box didn't give any clues. She carefully lifted the top of the box and then her eyes immediately welled up.

"Oh, Chase it's beautiful. You made this?" It was a wooden sign, painted pale blue with white nautical rope trim and white letters that said The Beach Plum Inn.

"It was actually a group effort. I cut the wood, Kate found the rope trim, Abby glued it on and Kristen did the painting."

Lisa looked around at all four of her children. "Thank you. It's the best gift you could have possibly given me."

"Now, let's just hope you get approved," Chase joked.

"They'd better approve you," Paige said. "I'll be at that meeting."

"I will too," Sue added.

"We'll all be there to support you, Mom," Kate said.

"When are you heading to Florida, Paige?" Lisa asked. Paige spent several months in Miami's South Beach every winter.

"A few days after the meeting. I can't wait. It's already getting much too cold here for my liking." Paige was originally from Florida and her parents still lived there. She hated the cold.

"Kate, I heard you might be staying here for a while. Your mom said you're going to be writing about the film festival. That sounds exciting," Sue said.

"I'll be here for at least a few months, maybe longer depending on if more work comes my way."

Paige looked thoughtful for a moment. "Do you have somewhere lined up to stay, once your mom opens for business?"

Kate laughed. "I'll probably be couch surfing, either on her living room sofa or crashing at Abby's. I'll figure something out."

Paige set her nearly empty champagne glass down and smiled. "Well, I have a better idea. Why don't you stay at my place? It's going to be empty until the end of April and I'd love to have someone there to check the mail and keep an eye on the place."

"Really? That would be perfect!" Kate looked thrilled

and Lisa thought it was a great idea too. Paige lived just a mile away.

"Great, it's a done deal! Let's toast to it!" Paige lifted her glass of Prosecco, and they all did the same. "Merry Christmas everyone!"

CHAPTER 5

Kate felt a sense of childlike wonder when she woke Christmas morning to see a thin blanket of fluffy white snow on the ground and snow swirling and twirling outside her window. The weather reports had predicted flurries, and it wasn't supposed to amount to much, but it was fun and festive to watch.

She slowly made her way downstairs. Her mother was already in the kitchen, baking the cinnamon walnut coffee cake that they had every Christmas morning. The rich smell of butter and sugar was in the air when Kate walked into the room. She made herself a cup of coffee and settled at the island, watching her mother work. She felt a little guilty just sitting there.

"Can I do anything to help?" she asked. Though she already knew what her mother's answer would be.

"I think I'm all set honey. The cake is almost done and there's really not much else to do. I made the green beans yesterday, the roast just needs to go into the oven along with the baked potatoes. The only thing I have left is to make the popovers, and I'll do that right before the roast is done." Every Christmas they always had the same meal, prime rib, though Kate's favorite thing was the Yorkshire pudding popovers. They were light and airy and melted in her mouth.

"Why don't you sit down and join me then? Have a cup of coffee and relax."

"I think I will."

While her mother was making a cup of coffee, Kate opened her laptop and brought up the Airbnb listing she was finalizing. When her mother sat down, she turned the laptop so that she could see.

"Tell me what you think of this?"

"Oh, you put the listing up already?"

"No, it's not live yet. Not until you give me the okay."

"Oh, good. You scared me there for a minute."

Kate waited while her mother looked over the ad. Kate thought she'd done a good job on it. She'd taken pictures of all the rooms, fully decorated and with their new bedding. She'd waited until the light was just right, to capture the beauty of the ocean views and sunshine. The rooms looked elegant and inviting.

"You've done a wonderful job, thank you. We should wait until after the board of selectmen's meeting though, shouldn't we?" The meeting was just over a week away.

"I say we put it up now, with the first date available a week from yesterday, so you might get some last minute visitors for New Year's Eve weekend."

Her mother looked hesitant. And Kate knew what was worrying her.

"It won't affect your chances with the board of select-men. As long as you don't put the sign up until you get approval, you're fine. Anyone can use Airbnb to rent out rooms. It might even help, if you can say you've rented some already."

"I suppose it wouldn't hurt to see if there's any interest."

Kate smiled. "Great, then all that's left to do is to hit the button." She pressed submit. "And now it's done. You're officially in business!"

Her mother took a slow sip of coffee. She looked thoughtful as she set her cup down. "Wouldn't it be some-thing if I'm able to rent out a room before then? It's prob-ably doubtful this time of the year, I would imagine."

"You never know. Lots of people on the Cape might want to get away for a long weekend but not go too far. Nantucket is perfect."

Chase, Kristen and Abby arrived around ten, and they all had coffee cake before exchanging gifts. They'd agreed to not go overboard this year and to just get one gift each as no one really needed anything. Everyone laughed when Kate and Kristen opened the gifts they'd gotten each other and saw that it was the exact same sweater—Kate had bought a white one for Kristen and she'd bought it in black for Kate. They had similar taste in clothes, but usually Kate would buy a sweater for Kristen and get one for herself too. It was kind of a running joke in the family.

They had a lovely, relaxing day and after eating their big meal, and helping their mother to clean up, Kate, Kristen and Abby decided to go for a walk on the beach.

The snow flurries had finally stopped and the ocean breezes had blown the light dusting of snow off the beach.

"Mom, are you sure you don't want to come with us?" Abby asked as they put on their coats and boots.

"No, I'm going to make a cup of tea and watch It's a Wonderful Life with Chase." Another of their holiday traditions.

"We won't be gone long, we'll join you when we get back," Kate said.

It was cold, but the air had stilled and the sun was shining as they walked down the long boardwalk to the beach. They decided to walk along the beach to the lighthouse which was about a mile away. It was a good walk, and Kate figured it would give them time to talk. She was worried about Abby. She'd been quiet and withdrawn since telling them that she was pregnant and thinking of getting divorced.

"How are you really doing?" Kate asked her as they walked.

"I'm okay. Hanging in there. It's harder than I thought it would be, not having Jeff in the house, especially at Christmas. He called this morning, and I agreed to see him tonight. He's going to stop by after he has dinner with his family."

"Are you exchanging gifts?" Kristen asked.

Abby nodded. "He said he has something for me. And I'd already bought his weeks ago."

"Are you ready to take him back?" Kate asked. She imagined it must be hard to exchange gifts and then go their separate ways.

But Abby shook her head. "No, I'm not ready. I need time. A lot of time, I think. It's barely been a week. And the holidays are so full of emotion, it's not normal everyday feelings. If I took him back now, I don't think anything would change. I don't think he gets it yet." She sighed as they continued to walk.

"Have you considered counseling?" Kristen asked.

"I hadn't, but Jeff asked me that this morning too, and I said that I'd be open to it. It can't hurt I suppose?"

"It might be a really good thing. To help you communicate better about what's really bothering you and maybe come up with a solution that works for both of you." Kate thought counseling might be a step in the right direction. She liked Jeff too, and it had felt strange that he wasn't with their family for Christmas.

"How are things going with Sean?" Abby asked Kristen.

"No change. He's at his ex's house today for Christmas dinner, with their son, Julian."

"He still spends a lot of time with his ex. Any updates on when his divorce will be finalized?" Kate asked.

Kristen laughed. "As far as I know, he hasn't even filed yet. They're still just separated."

"Oh. I didn't realize that. I thought you guys were getting more serious."

"Yeah, well, it's complicated I guess." Kristen sounded like she didn't really want to say more than that, so Kate changed the subject and told them about the Airbnb listing.

"I'll show it to you when we get back. It will be interesting to see if she gets any bites. I don't really know what to expect this time of year."

"I still think it's a strange idea. I know mom needs to make money somehow, and I know it's selfish of me, but I don't like it," Abby admitted.

"I've warmed up to the idea. I agree it will be strange, at least at first, but I think it might be good for her," Kate said.

They reached the lighthouse and turned around. Kate was glad for the walk, and it was fun chatting with her sisters. They both caught her up on all the island gossip.

"So, when do you start your freelance assignment?" Kristen asked. "The film festival sounds like a fun thing to write about."

"I have a meeting on Monday, actually. I'm interviewing Philippe Gaston."

"The Philippe Gaston? He's on the island already?" Abby asked.

"He bought a place a few years ago and spends most of his time here, when he's not flying to LA or somewhere for a filming project."

"He belongs to the same country club that Sean does," Kristen said. "He says he's a great golfer."

"Where does he live?" Abby asked.

"He has a beach house in 'Sconset. That's where I'm meeting him. I'm curious to see what it's like," Kate admitted. 'Sconset, short for Siasconset was one of the most exclusive areas on Nantucket.

"Is he still married to that actress?" Kristen asked.

"I'm not sure. I thought I read that they were getting divorced, but that was a while ago."

"He's hot, like seriously ridiculously handsome. Maybe he'll help you get over Dylan?" Abby grinned.

But Kate laughed at the idea of it. "That's the last thing I'm looking for. From what I've read, he's another Dylan type, and I don't need that. I am looking forward to talking to him though. He's enormously talented." Philippe was a New York Times bestselling author turned film producer and more recently, he'd been creating a TV drama series for Netflix.

She knew he'd started his career in journalism too, and she was curious to learn how he made the transition. A secret dream of hers was to write a novel, and she was thinking she could get started on it while she was on Nantucket for the winter. But, a part of her was terrified of the idea too, terrified of failure.

When they reached the house, the snow was beginning to fall softly again. Once they were inside and settled around the kitchen island with cups of hot cinnamon tea all around, Kate opened her laptop to show her sisters the listing on Airbnb. She was shocked to see that she had an email alert already.

"Mom, we have our first reservation!" she called out.

"We do?" Her mother paused the movie and joined them in the kitchen.

"A Rhett Byrne is arriving New Year's Eve and has booked a full week!" Kate announced excitedly.

"Well, isn't that something?"

KATE WAS ANNOYED TO FIND HERSELF FEELING A BIT

nervous as she drove down the long winding driveway that led to Phillip Gaston's oceanfront home. There was nothing overly intimidating about the house, it was lovely, with huge windows that overlooked the water. And it wasn't too big, unlike most of the homes on this street.

She parked out front, as he'd requested and gathered her tote bag with her notebook and voice recorder. She always liked to record her interviews whenever possible so she didn't have to worry about missing anything. She knew that she was nervous because she was such a fan of his work more than the fact that he was ridiculously handsome. She was pretty sure that Dylan had cured her of falling for someone like him.

She slowly walked to the front door and rang the bell. A moment later a slightly overweight guy about her age opened the door. He was wearing an apron and looked vaguely familiar and then she remembered how she knew him.

"Gary?" He was a friend of Abby's husband and had gone to school with them. He recognized her immediately.

"Hey, Kate. Good to see you." He opened the door wider, and she stepped in. "Philippe will be down in a minute. He asked me to get the door. Come on in."

She followed him to the kitchen where he had sheets of pasta spread out all over the kitchen counters and island.

"I didn't realize you worked for Philippe?"

"I'm just doing some personal chef work for him when he's on the island, depending on what's going on.

He's hosting a dinner tonight, for some Netflix execs that are in town for a few days."

"Netflix. Wow." Kate was impressed.

Gary smiled as he reached for his rolling pin. "I know, right? I'm hoping to wow them with my fresh lobster ravioli in Alfredo sauce."

"That sounds amazing. Are you still with the Straight Wharf?" It was one of Kate's favorite restaurants and was closed for the winter.

"Yeah, it's a good gig. Ten years now. And I do my personal chef stuff on the side. Summers are crazy." He chuckled. "Some of these people have me on call just to make peanut butter and jelly sandwiches—whatever they're in the mood for."

Kate smiled. That was how the other half lived on Nantucket. So many families that summered on the island were extremely wealthy. It was common for wives and children to stay all week, while their husbands worked in the city, running hedge funds or other insanely lucrative businesses and flew to their Nantucket homes for the weekends.

Too many owned breathtakingly gorgeous houses that sat empty except for the week or two they decided to take their vacation. These were the people who would hire a personal chef for their stay, to cater to their every whim even if it was as simple as a bowl of cereal or a sandwich.

"It looks like he appreciates what you're able to do?" Kate commented.

Gary grinned. "Yeah, he let me pick the menu."

Kate turned at the sound of footsteps coming down the hall. Philippe Gaston was walking toward her in faded jeans that fit his slim body perfectly. He was buttoning a crisp white shirt as he walked and his dark brown hair was still damp and a bit too long and wavy. He smiled and apologized for keeping her waiting. His French accent was charming.

"Oh, I didn't mind. Gary and I were catching up."

"You know each other?" He sounded surprised at first, then laughed. "Of course you do, you're both natives right? Would you like anything to drink? Coffee, water?"

"No, I'm good, thanks."

"Let's go into my office then." He led the way through the kitchen to a sunny room that faced the ocean. The walls were lined with bookcases and were overflowing with books, many of them leather-bound. A large L-shaped wooden desk sat in the corner and two comfortable looking black leather chairs faced it. He sat in one and gestured for her to sit in the other.

"So, tell me all about yourself," he said, once she was seated and had her notebook on her lap.

She smiled. "What do you want to know? I'm here to talk about you."

"Whatever you care to share. I like to get to know the people that I'll be working with."

"All right. Well, I grew up here, went to Boston College and got a job at Boston Style magazine after gradation. I've worked there ever since." She paused and then admitted, "Well, until recently. I'm not on staff there anymore, just freelancing."

He nodded. "I thought I read somewhere that the

magazine was bought by a big corporation based out of New York." She could see the sympathy in his eyes.

"Yes, so I'm shifting into doing freelance work and hoping to stay on Nantucket at least through the Winter. Maybe longer if I can find enough work. I do love it here," she added.

"It's the most beautiful place I've been to," Philippe said. "I knew, the first time I visited, over ten years ago, that I'd want to buy a home here." He stared out the window and looked lost in thought. They were both quiet for a moment. Kate decided it was time to get started with her first questions.

"How did you first become involved with the film festival? Oh, and do you mind if I record our conversation?"

He shook his head. "No, of course I don't mind. I was invited to participate when my first book was made into a film. That was quite a year. I've been involved with creating film or TV projects ever since."

Kate remembered that book. Lucky Girl was an edge of the seat psychological thriller that had won Oscars for best picture, screenplay adaptation, which Philippe had also written, and for best actress. Which was how he'd met his now ex-wife, Laura Smith.

"Do you have to travel a lot?" she asked.

Philippe ran his hand through his wavy hair and then he leaned forward. She tried not to notice how green his eyes were as he spoke. "Yes and no. I'm often here for months at a time, when I'm writing something new. But then, I might travel for several months, usually to LA where most of the shows are filmed. That's a lot of fun though." His face lit up, and she asked him to explain what he meant.

"Well, writing a book is great, you're in charge and it's totally your vision. Having that turned into a film is fantastic, but you have to be okay with your story changing and letting other people mold it to their vision." He paused before adding, "The writer is less important in film. But television, well, that's where all the power is for a writer."

Kate leaned forward, intrigued. "How is it different?" She didn't have any idea how the writer's role varied between the two mediums.

"Well, with TV, when it's my story being produced and I'm the show runner, I'm involved in just about everything except directing. For example, I happened to casually mention that I'd love to cast someone like Michael C. Hall, the actor that played Dexter." He paused and Kate nodded. She'd loved the show Dexter about the serial killer that only killed people that deserved to die.

"Well, they made it happen, and cast him for the lead. They've pretty much given me anything I've asked for, so far." He grinned and his expression reminded Kate of a mischievous teenage boy. "The money is also a lot better than writing books. I get a nice piece of the profits."

Kate glanced around the room and took in the luxurious leather and quality furnishings. Philippe was clearly doing very well for himself.

"That's interesting. I can see why you'd prefer it." Kate was quiet for a moment, and then found herself saying, "I was thinking that I might try to write a book too someday, maybe while I'm here this winter." She felt a bit silly admitting it as she was such a beginner compared to him.

But he seemed enthusiastic about the idea. "Oh, you should. You obviously can write. What genre are you thinking of?"

"Mystery. I've always enjoyed puzzle stories, and investigations."

He looked pleased with her answer. "Well, if you write it, I'd be happy to read for you and offer suggestions. I don't often do that. Only when I have a good feeling about someone, and I already know I like your writing."

"You're read some of my work?" Kate was both surprised and flattered.

"Yes. When I got your initial email, I searched online and read several of your features. I wouldn't have agreed to meet with you otherwise."

She nodded. It made sense that he would have checked her out ahead of time.

"Oh, well, thank you. So, tell me more about your involvement with the film festival."

They chatted for another half hour as Philippe told her all about his early days and how he was involved currently, which was mostly as a host for some of the screenings, since in recent years he'd been doing more television than film work.

"It's more a celebration of the medium than anything else, and a chance for some local folks to get noticed. It also brings people to the island which is always good for the economy." He smiled again, and she couldn't help thinking that he looked more like a movie star himself than a writer. He had deep dimples that appeared when he smiled along with laugh lines that only made him more attractive.

"It seems like more and more celebrities come for the festival every year," she commented.

He nodded. "It's amazing how many of the LA folks look forward to it. Nantucket is exotic to them and a breath of fresh air."

She closed her notebook. They'd covered everything she wanted to ask.

"Well, I think I have everything I need. Is there anything else you'd like to add?"

Philippe thought for a moment. "I can't think of anything. Though I do have a question or two." He smiled slowly and held her gaze. Kate suddenly felt her pulse quicken and glanced around the room until her eyes fell on the large clock. It was definitely time to go. She took a breath.

"Sure, what would you like to know?"

"How do you feel about lobster ravioli?"

She didn't make the connection, at first. "I like it."

"Good. I'm having a small gathering tonight. Why don't you join us? The director, the producer and a few other execs from my show will be here. You might find it adds some interesting color for your story."

The invitation both intimidated and intrigued her equally. She knew that it was a huge opportunity.

"I'd love to. Thank you."

"Fantastic, I'll see you back here at seven then."

"My jet-setting daughter," Lisa teased Kate as they sat in the kitchen drinking coffee while Kate told her all about her meeting with Philippe Gaston.

"I'm excited to go of course, but a little terrified too. What will I talk to these people about? And what will I wear?"

Lisa chuckled. "They're just people. And you're a reporter, just ask them questions."

Kate nodded. "You're right, of course. But there's still the matter of what to wear."

Lisa thought for a moment. "Do you have a simple black cocktail dress? You can't go wrong with basic black."

Kate relaxed a bit. "I do. I'll wear that."

Lisa took a sip of coffee and smiled. Her sensible older daughter was star-struck.

"What's he like? Is he as handsome as he looks on his book cover?"

"No, he's actually better looking if that's possible, and charismatic. And he has that accent. Fortunately, I'm immune to that kind of charm."

Lisa raised her eyebrows and Kate laughed. "He's interesting to talk to though and seems really nice. A good person to get to know."

"I asked around. Paige says his divorce was final a few months ago, and no one has seen him around town with anyone else. So, he seems available."

"Mom, I'm sure he wouldn't be interested! And I'm not looking, anyway. It's way too soon after Dylan." Her eyes looked pained and Lisa knew her daughter was still hurting, even though she put on a brave face.

"I'm just teasing you, honey. Go and have fun. At least you know the food will be good. I've had Gary's lobster raviolis and they're delicious."

CHAPTER 6

K ate returned to Philippe's house at ten past seven. There was a valet out front, and she shivered as she stepped out of her car and handed the young man her keys. The wind had picked up, and the air was cold. She pulled her long coat more tightly around her as she walked toward the front door.

This time when she knocked, the door was opened by Philippe himself, who welcomed her warmly.

"Thank you for coming. Come on in. You can hang your coat here." He indicated a closet to the left as they stepped inside. She slid her coat off and felt grateful that her black dress had long sleeves. It was warm, and the cut was elegant with a simple boat neck. At her waist it fell into a fuller skirt in a shimmery fabric that fell just below her knees. It was a pretty dress, and one that she felt comfortable in.

"You look lovely," Philippe said as he hung her coat in the closet and then led her into the main room where about a dozen people, mostly men and one older woman, were chatting and drinking cocktails while a young waitress circled the room, passing out appetizers. Kate was surprised to see a few familiar faces too. Richard Goodwin, who ran the local theater was there, and also Jack Trattel, which was interesting.

"What are you drinking?" Philippe asked as the server came toward them.

"I'd love a glass of wine, Chardonnay if you have it."

"Chardonnay it is." The server nodded and scurried off, returning a moment later with the wine and a tray of mini crab cakes. Philippe popped one in his mouth and encouraged her to do the same. She did, and it was delicious.

"I'll introduce you to everyone," he said as he led her over to a group of men.

Kate took a sip of her wine and followed. She tried to keep up as all the names went in one ear and out the other. Many of them, she'd heard before, or read about in the papers.

The last two people were Richard and Jack who were laughing as they walked toward them.

"I'm assuming you probably already know these characters," Philippe said lightly.

"I do."

"I'll let you catch up then. Looks like I'm being summoned to the kitchen. We'll be sitting down to eat soon. We'll talk more then." He walked off as Kate turned to Richard and Jack.

"I don't see you for years and then suddenly twice in two weeks," Jack said with a smile.

"I know, right? How do you know Philippe?"

"From playing poker."

"Poker?"

He nodded. "A few of us play now and then, mostly during the winter when it's quiet here. Philippe happened to stop by the seafood market right before closing one night, and we were down a guy, so I asked him to join us. We've been friends ever since. He'd just bought a place here and didn't know many people yet."

"So, you were being neighborly. That was nice of you."

Jack smiled. "Like I said, we were short a man. He's a decent guy though."

Kate turned to Richard. "It's nice to see you here too. How's Maryanne?" Richard's wife, Maryanne was a friend of her mother.

"She's fantastic. She was sorry she couldn't make it tonight. She's off-island visiting her sister for a few days."

Kate wondered where Jack's girlfriend, Cissie, was. "How's Cissie?" she asked.

Something she couldn't quite place, flashed across his face. "I assume she's fine. We're not together anymore."

"Oh, I didn't realize. I'm sorry." Kate felt like she'd created an awkward moment. But Jack didn't seem to mind.

"Don't be sorry. It's all good. It was a long-time coming."

"I just recently ended a relationship too," she admitted. "I'm looking forward to a relaxing winter and taking a break... from everything."

His eyes met hers and she saw a silent understanding in them. She relaxed and was glad that both Richard and

Jack were there. She'd never been one for making small talk with strangers.

They chatted easily, and a short while later, the server came by to invite them to head into the dining room. Philippe's table was a giant round one with twelve place settings. It was elegantly decorated with name cards by each oversized shimmery gold plate. Kate found her seat and was pleased to see that Jack was on her left and was surprised to see that Philippe was on her right.

Everyone took their seats and the next hour and a half was a delightful whirlwind of fascinating conversation and one decadent course after another. The lobster ravioli were as amazing as her mother had said and the sliced tenderloin with a red wine sauce melted in her mouth.

Philippe was a gracious host and kept the conversation lively and fun. He also made an effort to include Kate, asking her opinion on several subjects that came up as they debated what kind of storylines would resonate most with women. She assured them that killing off the beloved hero was not a good idea.

"More than anything, women want a happy ending," she said.

"But we have such a cool death scene that could happen next season," one of the execs said. "The special effects could be epic."

But Philippe shook his head. "I think Kate's right. We don't want to alienate half of our audience. We might not get them back."

Over coffee and dessert, Kate learned the reason why all the execs were in town. Philippe quietly told her that they were negotiating a long-term deal for him to create more shows over the next few years. And they were on hiatus now for a few months. The execs wanted to get a deal done before Philippe could say yes to a different project.

"That's exciting," she said.

"It is. It means I'll have a lot of free time over the next few months. I'll be working on a new book of course, but there are still nights and weekends. Maybe we can go out sometime? Grab dinner or see a movie?"

Kate was taken aback, both by the invitation and the uncertainty she saw in his eyes. As if he was worried she might say no. She couldn't refuse him, though she wasn't looking to date anyone, especially Philippe Gaston. But, she hoped they could be friends.

"That sounds fun. I'd love to."

"Good, I'll give you a call later this week to set something up."

Kate took a sip of her coffee and realized that Jack had heard their interchange. She turned to ask him a question, and he beat her to it.

"How's your mom? Are you staying with her while you're here?" he asked.

"She's great. I'll be staying with her for a while, but she's turning the house into a bed and breakfast, so I'll probably be moving out soon. Her friend Paige is heading to Florida for a few months, so I'm going to watch her house for her while she's gone."

"Paige Burton?" he asked.

She nodded. "Yeah, she lives a mile or so away from our house, on Sycamore Lane."

He grinned. "Well, it looks like we'll be neighbors then. I live a few doors down from her place."

"You do?"

"I bought the house three years ago and spent a year renovating before I moved in. Mine's the blue-gray one, same side as Paige."

"So, you're on the water too. I think I know which house you mean." It was a smaller house for the area, but plenty big enough for most people and had a huge, wrap around deck.

"Yeah. The house was a mess when I bought it, really run down. But the land and views are amazing. I built the biggest deck I could get away with and that's where I spend most of my time when the weather is good. There are stairs to the beach too. It's not good for swimming as it's kind of rocky, but it's great for fishing."

"Funny that we're going to be neighbors," Kate said.

"Yeah." He glanced at Philippe who was engrossed in an animated conversation. "I'd say you're settling in pretty well. He's newly single too by the way."

Kate felt herself flush a little. "I meant it when I said I wanted to take a break. I'm not looking to get into a relationship with anyone right now."

"Same here. Just taking things one day at a time. You never know what each day will bring."

"You're sounding philosophical," Philippe said. He'd caught Jack's last comment.

"Must be the time of year. With New Year's Eve around the corner and all," Jack said lightly.

"Right. That's not even a week away."

Kate didn't want to think about New Year's Eve, especially as there was no one in her life to kiss when midnight rang in the new year. She decided to change the subject.

"Do you ever go to the board of selectmen meetings?" she asked Jack and then looked at Philippe and added, "either of you?"

"I've never been to one. I avoid that kind of thing," Philippe said.

"I go once in a while, it depends what's on the agenda. Why do you ask?" Jack said.

"The next meeting is a week from today, and my mother is seeking approval to officially open her bed and breakfast and put a sign up."

Jack frowned. "What will she do if they say no?"

"She'll still open but won't put her sign up. She can rent rooms through Airbnb. But if they approve, she can also put up a website and advertise more heavily both on and off-island."

"There's really nothing in all of Beach Plum Cove area for hotels, or restaurants. Seems like an unmet need." Jack said.

"I know. They are looking to approve a new restaurant too. Someone is taking over the old one and reopening."

"No kidding? That place has been closed for years. It would be great to have it open again and good for your mother's business too. People could walk there."

"It would be perfect, but I'm a little nervous. You know how Nantucket can be sometimes."

"Yeah, they keep saying no to McDonald's and a few other businesses that people want. They are resistant to change."

"I do get it. They don't want to lose the charm that makes Nantucket unique. But I don't see how a bed and breakfast would jeopardize that."

"You probably have nothing to worry about then," Jack said.

"I hope not." But Kate was worried. She knew her mother needed this.

"I'm not busy Monday night. Maybe I'll stop by the meeting and lend my support," Jack said.

That was more than Kate expected. "Thank you, Jack. That means a lot."

———

KRISTEN SIGHED AND STRETCHED HAPPILY IN HER KING-sized bed. The sun streaming in through the windows had woken her, and she knew the light would be fantastic to finish the painting she was working on. She eased herself out of bed so that she wouldn't wake Sean. He was dead to the world though, so she needn't have worried.

They'd had a late night and Kristen was feeling hopeful again that she wasn't making a mistake by staying with him. They'd gone to one of their favorite restaurants, Basil's, a tiny place, where Sean knew the owner well and he sent over a round of drinks and a new appetizer he was testing for the menu.

After a leisurely dinner, they'd gone to hear some live music and then made their way back to her cottage where they fell into bed and it felt like the days when they'd first met. When Sean's focus was on her totally and he was romantic and loving. She'd wanted to ask him if anything had changed, if he'd finally filed for divorce, but she didn't want to break the mood.

She made a pot of coffee, and dove into her painting, losing all track of time once she began. Several hours later, she took a break and stood up to stretch. She'd been in the same position for so long that her muscles were protesting and she'd never even touched her cup of coffee. It was stone cold, so she dumped it out and made a new batch. She took her first sip as Sean made his way into the kitchen, still half-asleep.

"Want a cup? I just made it."

He nodded, and she poured him a cup and added a slug of heavy cream and extra sugar before handing it to him.

"Thank you. I need this." He leaned against the counter and took a slow sip.

"A little headache?" she teased him. She'd been fine because she rarely had more than two glasses of wine before switching to water or coffee. But Sean was an enthusiastic drinker and sometimes his Jack and Cokes went down so quickly that a hangover was inevitable.

"I keep meaning to have water, like you do."

She laughed. "Well, that helps, but drinking less is even more effective."

"Right."

"Are you hungry? I was about to make some eggs and toast."

He looked green at the mention of eggs.

"No, coffee is all I can handle."

"Think you'll be revived by tonight? We don't have to go out, we can get some takeout and stay in."

He looked at her in confusion. "Do we have plans tonight?"

"Well, I just assumed. It's New Year's Eve, Sean."

"I'm sorry. I have Julian tonight and I told his mother I'd stay for dinner."

Kristen said nothing for a long moment. Inside, she was seething. She tried to keep her voice calm and measured, though she felt like screaming at him.

"And you don't think that's a little odd, Sean? She invites you to stay for dinner on New Year's Eve?!"

He looked uncomfortable. "I didn't even realize what the date was. We'd never talked about New Year's Eve, so it wasn't on my mind."

"No, it doesn't seem like it was." Kristen slammed her coffee cup on the counter and splashed more coffee into it. She was suddenly exhausted on top of being furious as it finally sunk in that nothing was going to change with Sean. For whatever reason, he wasn't ready to completely let go of his marriage. And she felt like a fool. The only reason she'd agreed to date him in the first place was because he was separated and had told her he was getting a divorce ASAP.

"So, what, you're mad now?" Sean sounded frustrated. "I've told you before, I have to be careful about how I do this. I don't want to piss off Julian's mother. She could take me back to court and try to change our arrangement."

But she thought he was being dramatic and ridiculous.

"Why don't you just move back in with her? It would make things so much easier and save you a whole lot of money. I can't keep doing this Sean. I'm done." Her voice broke a little, betraying her emotions. She was close to tears.

He put his almost empty coffee mug in the sink and tried to wrap his arms around her. But she slithered out of his grasp, folded her arms across her chest and glared at him. She was afraid if he touched her, she'd cave or burst into tears.

Sean ran a hand through his hair in frustration as he paced around the room before stopping in front of her.

"What are you talking about? I thought we had a great time last night. I know I did."

"I had a wonderful time. Which is why I'm so upset right now."

"You were the one that said you didn't want to get serious," he reminded her.

"I said I wanted to keep things light, at first. I meant while you were married. But, you told me you were getting divorced."

"I am. It's just complicated. There's too much at stake to rush."

"Well, I certainly wouldn't want you to rush." Her voice dripped with sarcasm. He chose to ignore it and tried what had always worked in the past with her.

"I'm crazy about you, Kristen. I hate when we argue. I'll make this up to you, I promise. Let's go out tomorrow night instead. It's going to be packed everywhere tonight, anyway. Tomorrow we'll have the place to ourself. It will be more romantic. What do you say?" His eyes met hers and the smile that used to make her melt didn't have the same effect anymore. But she was done fighting with him. She just wanted him to go.

"I don't know. I need to get back to work."

He took that as a win and grinned. "I'll call you tomorrow."

As soon as he left, and the house was empty, Kristen let the tears come. She didn't cry for long though. She was more angry than sad, and she was done crying over him.

CHAPTER 7

No one was in the mood to celebrate on New Year's Eve. Lisa and Brian had usually just gone out for a quiet dinner or to an occasional house party. But since he'd passed, she hadn't done much of anything. It was just another night to her.

But this year, she sensed that the girls weren't in the mood to do much either, and her natural inclination was to try to lift their spirits. She'd invited them over and planned to put in an early order for takeout at their favorite Chinese restaurant. She figured they could stay in and watch movies and maybe if they were still awake, they could watch the ball drop. She thought it would be her, Abby, and Kate, but when Kristen called to let them know Sean cancelled their plans at the last minute, Lisa insisted that she join them as well.

She was also a bit nervous as the clock approached three in the afternoon. Her first guest, Rhett Byrne was due to arrive any moment. He was going to be staying in ACK, the largest room, and she fussed around in the morning making sure it was perfect for him. She put extra blue-gray towels in the bathroom, set several bottles of water on the nightstand and a box of chocolate covered cranberries for a snack. They were made at the local chocolate shop and were a great taste of the island, fresh cranberries wrapped in silky dark chocolate.

She left a local newspaper on the table by the window and gave the bedspread a final smoothing. She also left a note welcoming him and leaving the number to her cell phone in case he needed anything at anytime. She was curious about why he wanted to stay for a whole month. It was an odd time to take such a long vacation.

Kate had told her to google him, to find out more about him, and she'd meant to do that, but hadn't gotten around to it until this morning. It had felt a bit intrusive, but finally her curiosity had gotten the best of her. From what she saw in the quick search she did, he owned several restaurants, one in New York City and two in Boston, as well as one in Palm Beach. Maybe he was visiting friends that owned a restaurant here or maybe he just wanted to get away. Nantucket in the winter was great if you didn't want anyone to bother you.

People used to always ask Lisa how she could stand being on the island in the winter when it was so quiet and all the tourists were gone. The implication was that it must be horribly boring. But Lisa found it anything but. She loved the off-season on Nantucket, and she knew many of her friends felt the same way.

As much as they appreciated the tourists that helped the island economy, it was also a bit of a relief when the crowds died down and they had the island back to themselves again. Lisa never minded the cold or the long winters. It just made her appreciate the summers even more. And in the winter, people weren't as busy, so she saw some of her friends more often, and caught up on her reading too.

At three o'clock sharp, she heard a car pull into the driveway. There was plenty of parking, and she had emailed instructions for Rhett to park in the open paved area to the right of the garage. There was room for three cars there. A few minutes later, she heard a knock on the door and went to let him in.

She opened the door and took a step back to look up at the very tall, big man standing there. He was several inches over six feet and had lots of thick, sandy hair with streaks of gray. He smiled when he saw her and it was an easy, friendly smile that lit up his tanned, weathered face. She guessed his age to be a little older than hers, maybe closer to sixty?

"You must be Rhett Byrne?"

"That's me!"

"Come on inside, and I'll get your key." She led him into her living room and went to her roll top wooden desk that was along the wall. She kept all of her business things there, stamps, bills, extra keys. She found the keys to ACK and turned to him.

"I'll show you to your room. Did you have a long trip to get here?" She wondered if he was coming from Boston or New York.

"Not too bad. I didn't hit too much traffic coming from Boston, but the ride over was longer, because I brought my car." The fast ferry was only an hour, but the bigger boat that carried vehicles, the one they'd nick-named the slow boat, took over two hours.

Rhett followed her up the stairs, and she opened the door to his room and handed him the keys. He stepped inside and looked around while she found herself holding her breath, hoping he'd like it. He stepped toward a window and took in the view of the beach. And then he smiled.

"This is better than I expected. Thank you."

"If you need anything, give me a call. Breakfast is from eight until ten. Just head to the dining room when-ever you're ready. You can help yourself to coffee and there will be cold cereals, fruit and pastries and I'll bring in something hot as well."

"I'll do that, thanks."

"Are you here on vacation?" She knew she was being nosy, but she was curious and thought she should make a little conversation. It seemed rude to just show him to his room and walk away after barely talking to the man.

He laughed. "I wish. But I'm going to try to make it a working vacation. I have friends here on the island. They insisted I come in today to go to their New Year's Eve party. It's the last thing I feel like doing, but it's probably smart of me to go."

"Oh, why is that?"

"It's a good chance for me to meet more people on the island. And to up my chances of having the board of selectman approve my new restaurant. They say it's a formality really as the sale of the building is contingent on my getting that license, and I know they want the sale to go through."

"Oh! I didn't realize that. I'll be at the meeting too. I'm seeking approval to make this an official bed and breakfast."

"I wouldn't think they'd give you a problem about that. But you never know." He glanced around the room and Lisa sensed he wanted to settle in.

"I'll leave you to it. Don't hesitate to call if you need anything."

"Thank you."

"So, what's he like?" Kate asked as Lisa helped herself to an egg roll. The girls had all arrived within minutes of each other and they were sitting around the kitchen island eating Chinese food off paper plates. Kristen had opened a bottle of champagne and also brought some sparkling apple juice for Abby so she wouldn't feel left out.

"He seems very nice. He's a big man, a bit older than me."

"Is he handsome?" Kristen asked.

"He is actually."

"Married?" Abby asked.

"I don't know."

"Mom, how can you not know? Was he wearing a wedding ring?" Kate sounded exasperated.

Lisa laughed. "I don't know. I didn't think to look." It was true. She didn't make a habit of noticing if men were wearing wedding rings.

"You really should start paying attention to these

things." Kristen smiled as she reached for more chicken lo mein. "Have you considered dating?"

Lisa almost dropped the chicken finger she'd just picked up.

"Dating? No. It hasn't crossed my mind. It hasn't been that long since I lost your father."

The girls exchanged glances and then Kate spoke.

"Mom, it's been over three years. And you're still young. I'm not saying go on Match.com, but maybe just be more aware and open."

Lisa felt uncomfortable having this conversation with her daughters. She knew they meant well, but she wasn't in any hurry to date anyone.

"I'm not making any promises, but I will start paying more attention, how's that?"

"That's perfect," Abby said, and the others nodded in agreement. Lisa decided to change the subject

"How are things going with you and Jeff?"

"He wanted to take me out tonight, but I told him I wasn't up to it. New Year's Eve is such a party night, and it just didn't feel right. I can't drink, not that it matters that much, but I've also been so tired that I'll probably be yawning and ready for bed by nine."

"Why don't you meet for dinner another night soon?" Lisa suggested.

"I think we're going to do that. He said that he wants to cook dinner for me."

"He does? I didn't know Jeff knew how to cook?" Kristen laughed.

"As far as I know, he doesn't. So, it should be interesting."

"At least it sounds like he's making an effort," Lisa said.

Abby nodded. "I know. I'm hoping it's a step in the right direction."

"And Kate has a date coming up soon, with a celebrity, that famous writer with the good hair," Kristen said teasingly.

Lisa and Abby both looked at Kate. It was the first that Lisa had heard about a date. Kate immediately made light of it.

"It's not really a date. When I interviewed him, he invited me back that evening for a dinner with some people he works with at Netflix, and he mentioned going out sometime. But it might have been all talk. I haven't heard anything further from him."

"He reminds me a bit of Dylan," Kristen said slowly. "He has that same kind of charisma about him, you almost can't help but stare when he comes into the room. I see him out now and then at some of the local artist events. And now that I think about it, he's always with a date. I don't think I've ever seen him with the same woman more than once or twice."

"And that's why I really don't have any serious interest in dating him. If he does call me, I'll go out with him, but I don't want anything romantic. I do think he'd be an interesting person to get to know better though." Kate took a sip of champagne before adding, "Jack Trattel was at the party too."

"From Trattel's Seafood?" Kristen sounded surprised.

"He said they're poker buddies."

"Jack lives on the same street as Paige. She mentioned

that he moved in a year or so ago. He did a great job renovating his house. It's cute as could be." Lisa had noticed the transformation each time she went to visit Paige.

"He told me about that. Said we're going to be neighbors. It will be nice to know someone else nearby as most of the people on her street are away in the winter."

"And you'll be just a mile away from here too," Lisa reminded her.

After they finished eating, and put everything away, they collapsed in the living room and watched When Harry Met Sally, which they'd all seen multiple times but everyone loved it. As Abby had predicted, she started yawning just before nine and decided to head home.

"Are you sure you don't want to stay over? There's plenty of room if you don't feel like driving."

But Abby stood and pulled on her coat. "I'll be home in about ten minutes, and I'm exhausted and ready to fall into my own bed. I'll talk to you tomorrow, and I'll see all of you Monday night at the meeting."

After she left, Kristen stood up.

"Well, I will stay over, and I'm going to have a little more champagne. Anyone else ready for some?" She refilled her glass and added more to Kate's and Lisa's as well.

And then she raised her glass and made a toast. "To a wonderful new year and new beginnings for all of us."

"I'll drink to that!" Kate laughed and took a sip of champagne. Lisa did the same and wondered what new beginning Kristen was referring to for herself.

"Has anything changed with Sean?" she asked.

"No. Nothing has changed at all. Which is why everything is going to change. He doesn't realize it yet, but we're done. I'm telling him tomorrow."

———

LISA GOT UP EARLY THE NEXT DAY. SHE DECIDED TO make a Quiche Lorraine as her first hot meal. She figured that Kate and Kristen would have some too, so it wouldn't go to waste and it was one of her favorite dishes. She rolled a pie crust into a dish and poured in the creamy custard filling, cheese, sauteed onion and crispy bacon. An hour in the oven and it would be ready. She'd already stocked the dining room with coffee, tea and a Keurig machine so guests could make a single cup at a time.

At about a quarter to eight, she slid the quiche out of the oven and set it on an iron rack to cool. The crust was browned perfectly, and the smell was heavenly. Her stomach rumbled a bit, and she made herself a piece of toast to take the edge off. She wondered if Rhett was an early bird or if he'd sleep in and make his way down closer to ten, if at all. For all she knew, he might decide to skip breakfast entirely.

But at a quarter past eight, she heard steps outside the door and went to check the dining room. Rhett had found the coffee selection and was brewing a cup.

"Good morning," she said brightly. "I'll be right in with the quiche. Or if you don't like that, there's fresh fruit in that small refrigerator, and bagels and cereal on the counter."

"Quiche sounds great. I'll probably have a bagel too."

"Cream cheese is in the refrigerator if you need it." Lisa went and got the Quiche and carefully carried it into the dining room and set it on a hot plate she'd plugged in earlier. She'd cut the quiche into slices and told him to help himself.

"Did you eat yet?" He asked as he slid a piece of quiche onto his plate.

His question took her by surprise. "No, not yet."

"Would you like to join me? I'd love the company."

Her stomach rumbled again, and she laughed. "Sure. I'd like that." She made herself a second cup of coffee and joined him at the table along with her own plate of quiche.

"This is excellent," he told her after he took his first bite, and she was pleased to hear it.

"Did you have fun at your party?" He must have stayed out late as she never heard the front door open. She and the girls had gone to bed soon after the ball dropped.

"I did. It was a good time. And a late night. I hadn't seen most of these people in years and there was a lot to talk about. Most of them are excited about the restaurant."

Something about the way he said it got her attention. "Most of them? You mean some aren't excited?"

"Well, a few people seem to feel that there are already enough restaurants on the island. Adding another cuts into their profits. Or so they say."

"Oh, it was other restaurant owners that have an issue with you opening? Will that be a problem, do you think?"

She wondered if those people would be at the meeting Monday night.

"It had better not be. If they ran a better business, they wouldn't have anything to worry about." He spoke confidently, and she sensed that he knew his business well. She supposed he must if he had several successful restaurants.

"Hopefully, if they do speak up, it won't matter much. This area does need a restaurant."

"I agree." He grinned. "And a bed and breakfast. Do you have a name picked out?"

"The Beach Plum Cove Inn."

He nodded. "I like it. Simple and descriptive."

"Thank you. What happens if you do get approved? Will you need to do much to the restaurant to get it ready to open?"

"I'll start pulling permits right away and hire workers to get the renovation done. I've already got the plans all drawn up. It's not too extensive really, just an update on what's there and a slight reconfiguration to better use the space. I'm going to add more outside seating too and enlarge the deck."

Lisa could picture the outside of the restaurant. It wasn't on the water, but sat on a bluff and had an ocean view. It would be lovely to sit outside on the deck and look at the water while having dinner.

"Now I understand why you're planning to stay a whole month."

He laughed. "About that. I'd actually like to extend my stay for at least two more months if all goes well at the meeting Monday night. I didn't want to book that far out until I knew for sure."

"Oh! Of course it's all right."

"Fantastic. And if all your breakfasts are this good, I'm going to have to start taking long walks on that beach. Actually, I probably should do that, anyway."

Lisa laughed. "I won't make rich dishes every day, mostly just on the weekends. But definitely explore the beach, it's great for walking." She noticed that his plate and cup were empty and she quickly took her last bite and stood up. She didn't want to keep him from his day.

"There's plenty of quiche if you'd like more."

"I would, but I should pass. I'm going to go take that walk now, actually. Thanks for joining me for breakfast."

He stood, and she watched him go as she cleared the dishes. She'd enjoyed sharing breakfast with him and was excited that he might extend his stay. The steady money would be welcome and if all of her guests were this pleasant, she was going to enjoy running a bed and breakfast.

CHAPTER 8

Lisa changed clothes several times Monday night, trying to decide on the most appropriate outfit for the board of selectmen's hearing. She finally settled on charcoal gray dress pants, a crisp white shirt and a navy wool button down sweater. Matching pearl earrings and a necklace completed the look.

Kate rode with her to town hall where the evening meeting was going to be held.

"Don't be nervous," Kate said as they walked toward the entrance.

But Lisa couldn't help feeling jittery as they entered the room and looked around to find seats. It was early, but the room was filling up fast. Rhett was already there in the front row and waved them over. There were two empty seats next to him, and Kate started walking toward him. Lisa wasn't sure she wanted to sit in the front row, but she was glad for Rhett's support. They sat, and she introduced Kate to him.

"This is my first time attending one of these meetings," Kate said.

"First for me too," Rhett said and then added, "The crowd is bigger than I expected. It might make for an interesting evening."

His comment didn't help Lisa's nervousness any. Did a large turnout mean people would be more likely to object?

In the next fifteen minutes, the room filled completely until there was standing room only. Lisa was relieved and grateful to see that all of her children were there, though seated in the back of the room. And both Paige and Sue were back there too. She recognized quite a few familiar faces, people she knew or knew of.

At seven o'clock sharp, the selectmen took their places at the front of the room and the chairman called the meeting to order. They talked for nearly an hour, going over old business and pending issues before they finally got to the two requests for approval.

First up was Rhett's restaurant. Tom Goodwin, who was also an attorney, gave a summary of the request, the history of the restaurant and Rhett's plans to improve the building and transfer the liquor license. When he concluded, he asked the crowd, "Does anyone have an objection to voice about this request?"

When several people raised their hands and then stood to speak, Lisa worried for Rhett's chances, wondering how much weight the objections would carry. One was from Ben Hardy, who ran the nearest restaurant, which was in the next village over, more than five miles away. She could understand his concern as a lot of his business likely came from Beach Plum Cove. Yet, as a resident, she welcomed a new restaurant closer to home.

The other person objecting was Gladys Monroe who owned a summer home a few doors down from the restaurant. She was worried about noise and the impact on traffic. The selectmen allowed Rhett to respond, and he did so eloquently.

"Mr. Hardy, I can appreciate your concerns, but there already was a restaurant at this location, so the precedent is there, and I've talked to many local residents who welcome a place to go closer to home."

He then addressed Gladys Monroe, "This will be a family restaurant, not a nightclub. We won't have entertainment, so there shouldn't be any noise issues as we'll also close by ten at the latest. Regarding traffic, I'll speak again to precedent. My research shows that there was never a negative impact on traffic when the restaurant was open previously. I hope this addresses your concerns." He looked around the room and back at the selectmen before taking a seat.

Tom Goodwin addressed the room. "We will have a short discussion and then a vote on the matter." They spoke for just a few minutes before voting and unanimously agreed to approve Rhett's restaurant.

"Congratulations," Lisa said softly.

"Thank you. Your turn now."

"Next up we have a request from Lisa Hodges to operate a bed and breakfast out of her home. The name of the business would be The Beach Plum Cove Inn, with five rooms to rent. She is planning to be open year-round. She has no experience in hospitality and has not worked in over thirty years. There are no other such businesses in Beach Plum Cove. Are there any objections to granting this request?"

Lisa was surprised and dismayed to see three women raise their hands. One of them was Lillian Hardy, wife of Ben Hardy, the man who objected to Rhett's restaurant. Lillian ran a bed and breakfast out of their home, which was located next door to her husband's restaurant.

"There is no need for another bed and breakfast. Ours is right over the town line, and we are more than able to meet the demand for this area. Adding another bed and breakfast would be too much. It's simply not needed, and it's not fair to existing businesses." Lisa had never particularly cared for Lillian. She was one of those people who seemed to know everyone's business and had an opinion about it.

"Thank you, Lillian. Dawn Jacobs, it's your turn to speak."

Dawn was Lillian's mother and lived with them. She was in her eighties and had perfectly coiffed white hair cut into a chin-length bob. She was beautifully dressed and tiny, barely five feet tall. But she had a presence about her, and she wasn't the least bit shy or afraid to state her opinion.

"I have to agree with my daughter. There's simply no need for this business in Beach Plum Cove. There are plenty of fine hotels and lovely bed and breakfasts that already exist. Why should their businesses suffer?"

"Ms. Jones, you have the floor." Violet Jones, a stunning woman in her late thirties with long, blonde hair stood and looked around the room.

"I'm against this business. I live a few doors down from Lisa Hodges and I'm not keen on the idea of more traffic on our street and strangers coming and going at all hours. Beach Plum Cove is a lovely village and there's simply no need for this kind of thing here."

"Mrs.Hodges, you may have the floor to address these concerns."

Lisa stood slowly and hoped her nerves wouldn't get in her way. She took a deep breath and looked around the room.

"Part of the reason I decided to do this is that there is no place to stay in Beach Plum Cove. The nearest hotel or bed and breakfast is Lillian Hardy's business. But that's five miles away, and it's a long walk to our beach from there." Lillian sniffed and glared as Lisa spoke but Lisa didn't back down.

"My home is on the water with a private beach. Guests that stay with me will have access to that and there are very few bed and breakfasts that are actually on the ocean. Most of them are downtown. I believe that there is a demand for what The Beach Plum Cove Inn could offer. Regarding Violet's concerns, I am only planning to rent five rooms, it should have little to no impact on traffic."

"Is there anyone else with any concerns or who wish to speak in support of this request?"

Lisa was surprised when Rhett raised his hand. When told he could speak, he stood and addressed the room.

"I'm in favor of granting this request. I'm currently

renting one of Mrs. Hodges rooms and it's lovely. Her breakfast is wonderful and you can't beat the location. Another thing to consider is that she doesn't need your permission to rent her rooms out. She can do that simply by listing them on Airbnb. She would like to be able to put a sign up and advertise her business which she cannot do unless you approve her request. Thank you."

"All right. Thank you all. We will discuss and have an answer for you shortly."

Lisa waited, on pins and needles while the board discussed her request. When they voted, it was three for and four against. Kristen looked distressed and reached over to grab her hand and gave it a squeeze. Lisa was frustrated and confused. How could they vote against her business?

Tom Goodwin stood and addressed the room. "The board has decided at this time not to grant Lisa Hodges' request. Since, as Rhett stated, she can still operate her business via Airbnb, the board feels that would be a good first step, to see how that goes before granting full approval to make her home an official bed and breakfast. Thank you all for attending tonight and for making your voices heard."

"So, that's it then?" Kate looked furious as they stood to leave.

"They'll grant it eventually," Rhett said. "My guess is a few of the board members are friends with the Hardys and while they agreed to my request, it looks like they are listening to the Hardys' by denying yours. Just keep doing what you're doing. Even without the official sign, I expect you'll do just fine by listing with Airbnb. As you said, you're one of the few bed and breakfasts that is actually on the beach."

"I suppose so," Lisa said. It wasn't the outcome that she'd hoped for. But she wasn't ready to give up yet. With Rhett staying for more months and any other business Airbnb might send her way, she still felt as though her bed and breakfast could be a good thing.

"Well, this is a disappointment. But I have an idea," Kate said.

"What is it?"

"I don't want to say too much, in case it doesn't work… but I may have a way to get the word out without actually advertising."

A WEEK LATER, LISA WAS FEELING A BIT DISCOURAGED that there had been no further reservations or even inquiries from Airbnb. She'd checked her email every morning. But she reminded herself that it wasn't exactly the high season on Nantucket. Still, she thought she would have received at least one inquiry, even if it was for future dates during the Summer.

So, she decided not to check her email before settling down to breakfast. She didn't want to start the day feeling disappointed. Instead, she would enjoy sharing her morning meal with Rhett. She ate with him most mornings now. He was an early riser and was usually in the dining room a little past eight am. And he always asked her to join him. He said he welcomed the company and truth be told, she enjoyed talking to him too.

This morning, she'd made an egg white scramble with peppers and onions and chicken and apple sausage. It was healthy and tasty and Rhett went back for a second helping, which made her happy. While he was refilling his plate, she turned on her phone and it beeped indicating that she had new emails. She clicked and read through them and was pleasantly surprised to see not one but three reservation requests from Airbnb. Two were for Summer dates, but one was for the following week. A couple that was going to be arriving from England.

"What do you look so happy about? Some good news arrive by email?" Rhett teased her as he sat down.

"Yes, actually." She told him about the new reservations and then laughed as her phone beeped again with another reservation for the following month.

"I'm not sure where all this is coming from," Lisa said as Kate walked into the room and made herself a coffee. She had caught her mother's comments and looked pleased as she sat down to join them.

"You've gotten some interest?" she asked.

"Yes. Is this from something you've done?"

Kate nodded. "I wasn't sure if it would work, but had a feeling that it might. I wrote up a press release and a blog post and emailed some friends I know in the Boston area. They helped to spread the word, publishing the press release and sharing the blog post where I told all about your Nantucket bed and breakfast and how you were denied by the board, yet had oceanfront rooms available to rent. And I included a link to your listing on Airbnb."

"Thank you. Whatever you did worked." She told Kate about the flurry of reservations that had come in.

"Good, I'm glad to hear it. I also looked into this a bit more, and you can bring this up again in a few months. So, you might still be approved before the busy season hits."

"That would be ideal." Lisa laughed. "And maybe by then, I'll know what I'm doing. I'll have more experience."

"I think you're doing just fine. You're a natural." Rhett said and Lisa felt warm inside. She was growing to enjoy his company, and she'd noticed that he didn't wear a wedding ring. She'd googled him again and learned that he'd been married twice. He divorced his second wife about five years ago and had two adult children that both lived in New York City.

"What are you up to today, honey?" Lisa asked as Kate got up to take a cinnamon raisin bagel out of the toaster.

"I'm heading to the library to work on a new project. I'm going to look through some of the old newspaper archives to research the island's history of murders."

"Murders? Is that for a new assignment?" Lisa knew that Kate had turned in her feature on the film festival just the day before.

"No, though Amanda said she will have something else for me by the end of the week. I thought that I might try my hand at writing a murder mystery."

Lisa knew that Kate had always wanted to write a book.

"I think that's great! Will you set it on Nantucket then?"

"Yes. They say you should write about what you know. I thought I could maybe find an interesting old murder and base a story around it."

"Stories set on Nantucket seem to sell pretty well. I've bought a few myself," Rhett said. "I like to read the occasional mystery."

"I do too. I'm excited to see what you come up with, Kate."

"What are you up to today?" Kate asked.

"Laundry. I'm meeting Sue for a late lunch and I'm going to try to make a yoga class at four."

"You don't have to do laundry right now, do you?" Rhett asked.

"I could do it later, I suppose. Why do you ask?"

"You asked me about the renovation yesterday, and I'm heading over there now to see how the hardwood floors are coming along. I'd love to show you what I have planned, if you feel like taking a ride."

Lisa hesitated for a moment until Kate spoke up.

"That sounds like fun. You should go, Mom."

Lisa stood quickly, "Of course. I'd love to."

She followed Rhett to his truck and climbed into the passenger side. It was a work truck, but it was nicer than most, with soft, leather seats, and she caught a sweet hint of vanilla from the air freshener dangling from his rear view window.

It was a beautiful day, sunny and clear though cold.

Typical January weather on the island. The restaurant wasn't even a mile away, and they pulled up just a few minutes later. The building was a classic Cape Cod style with weathered gray shingles and white wooden shutters on all the windows. Lisa was impressed by the new deck which was very big and according to Rhett was just finished two days ago

"It's beautiful. I can't believe it went up so fast."

He grinned. "I was pretty optimistic about my chances and had these guys all lined up to start working the next day. Come inside."

She followed him in and looked around, trying to picture how it might look when it was finished. The room was large and open. Three guys were finishing laying the hardwood floors and she and Rhett were standing on the section that was already finished. The dark wood looked to be of high quality and glistened as the sun came through the windows and fell upon it.

"The flooring is lovely."

"Isn't it? I have this same wood at my Boston restaurants too." Rhett walked her all around the room, explaining what his plans were.

"I'm going to make these windows bigger, to let in more light and capture more of these gorgeous views. This is really a great spot, don't you think?"

Lisa smiled. His enthusiasm was contagious. "It is. I was sad when it closed."

"Once people try my food, this place is going to take off. The location is great, but it's the food that will bring them back." He was confident and Lisa believed him. She looked forward to the restaurant opening.

"How soon do you think you'll be ready to open?" It still looked a long way away from being done to her. But, she knew that things often moved fast as they got near the end.

"The goal is April. I want to be open for Daffodil weekend." The Daffodil Festival was held near the end of April and many viewed it as the official kick off weekend to the summer season. There were events all weekend, among them an antique car parade and tailgate picnic. It would be a big weekend on the island and if word got out that the restaurant would be open, Lisa imagined that they might be quite busy with both locals and visitors who were curious to check the new place out.

"That's a great idea."

"I have an antique car I'll bring over for it too and park it right out front. It's a real beauty. A 1966 Jaguar roadster. My daughter said she'd drive it down for me."

"Oh, it will be nice for you to see her."

"Alex is a great girl. She manages my flagship restaurant in Manhattan."

"Does your other daughter work there too?" She knew that they both lived in New York City.

"No, Jess is an attorney. She just got engaged a few weeks ago."

"How exciting." Lisa liked how Rhett's face lit up when he talked about his daughters.

"I like the guy she's engaged to. She's known him since law school and he's already almost part of the family. She might have the wedding here, if I can talk her into it. I'd give my chances about fifty-fifty," he said.

A half hour later he dropped her off at the house and

was going to head back to the restaurant. Before she got out of the car, Lisa impulsively invited him to join her and Kate for dinner.

"If you don't have plans of course. I have a beef stew simmering in the crock pot and it's much more than Kate and I can eat."

"You had me at beef stew." Rhett grinned. "Thank you for the invite. I'd love to join you both."

CHAPTER 9

The smell of bread baking wafted upstairs to Kate's bedroom, and she smiled. Her mother had nervously told Kate earlier that she'd invited Rhett to dinner, and Kate thought it was a great idea. Kate liked Rhett and thought he might be good company for her mother and if it turned romantic, well even better.

Rhett was night and day different from her father. Brian had been more of an indoors guy, not very good at building things or fishing or anything overly physical. She knew her parents had a good marriage though, except for the gambling addiction that her father had somehow managed to hide.

In retrospect though, she realized that they'd never thought much of it because her father acted like going to the casino was a fun hobby and he always spoke of winning or occasionally losing very small amounts, so it was all in good fun. When in actuality, he'd sometimes lost very large amounts, but hid his losses with lies and a smile.

If anything, Kate thought these next few months might be good for her mother. Spending some time with Rhett even it was strictly as friends, might help her transition into actually dating again. Meanwhile, Kate was trying to figure out what to wear for a date that she didn't really want to be a date.

Philippe had called a few days ago and left a message inviting her to go with him to the opening of a new art gallery. The owner, Andrew Everly, was from New York City and used to summer on Nantucket growing up. The name wasn't familiar to Kate, but she thought that Kristen might know of it. But she'd never heard of him either. When Kate had wavered about whether to accept the invitation, Kristen had insisted that she go so that she could get the inside scoop on the new place, but also to give Philippe a chance. She reminded her that it was just a first date, and there didn't have to be a second one.

Kate decided to wear her favorite black dress pants and a long, pale blue cashmere sweater with a simple white top layered under it. She ran a curling iron through her hair to give it some loose waves, pulled on her leather boots and she was ready to go. She popped into the kitchen on her way out and saw that Rhett had just arrived and was leaning against the kitchen island as her mother poured wine for both of them. She looked up when she heard Kate come in.

"Oh, you look nice, honey."

She handed Rhett his wine. "Kate won't be joining us for dinner, she has a date tonight."

"Well that sounds more fun than dinner with us," Rhett said.

Kate laughed. "I don't know about that. Mom's beef stew is amazing, and I could smell the bread baking from upstairs."

"I could too. I was very happy to follow the smell and appreciate the invitation." Rhett smiled at her mother as Kate checked the time. She needed to get going.

"Have a good night. I'll see you later."

PHILIPPE HAD OFFERED TO PICK HER UP, BUT KATE told him that she'd meet him at the gallery. They lived in opposite directions and the gallery was in the middle, downtown by the pier. Plus, Kate liked driving herself as it gave her more control on when she was able to leave.

Parking was always an issue on Nantucket though. Kate managed to find a spot in the main lot closest to the pier. She saw Philippe waiting outside the gallery. He waved when he saw her. It looked like a good crowd had already gathered. The building was two old gift shops that had been renovated and combined into one gallery.

"I thought we'd grab a bite to eat at the Club Car after we roam around here a bit," Philippe said as they walked inside.

"That sounds perfect." The Club Car was one of Kate's favorite restaurants, and it was just a short walk from the gallery.

Kate's first thought as they began to walk slowly around the room, looking at the paintings was that she wished Kristen could see it. It was a beautiful space, with all white walls and exposed brick that had also been painted white so that all the colors of the paintings stood out.

A server came by offering flutes of champagne. Philippe took two and handed one to her. As they continued to walk around, a few other servers drifted by carrying trays of stuffed mushrooms and spanakopita. The little phyllo pillows stuffed with spinach and cheese were delicious. Kate only had one of each though so she wouldn't ruin her appetite for dinner.

"Kate, this is Andrew Everly. We were just admiring the gallery. You've done a great job here." Andrew was as tall as Philippe and a bit leaner. His hair was almost black and his eyes a pretty hazel that popped against his light skin. Kate guessed he had some Irish in his background, maybe. He had an artsy look about him, with a black t-shirt, blazer, jeans and black-rimmed glasses.

"Thank you." Andrew held his hand out and Kate shook it. "It's nice to meet you Kate."

"Andrew and I met in college. We both went to NYU. He's the one who first introduced me to Nantucket."

Andrew nodded. "My parents have a place here and we came for the first film festival, over a long weekend. Philippe is the one who told me about this building when it became available."

Kate was intrigued. She hadn't realized they were such good friends. "Will you be living here year-round? Or splitting your time between here and New York? Do you have a gallery there too?"

"I have several actually. But they are well established

now, and I have good people that work for me, so I don't have to be there all the time. I'll be going back and forth as needed. But, I hope to be here for long stretches of time."

They chatted for a few minutes and Kate liked Andrew quite a bit. She noticed that he wasn't wearing a ring and couldn't help thinking that she'd love for Kristen to meet him. She hoped that Kristen really was serious about ending things with Sean. It sounded like she was, but Kate had heard it before, and Kristen hadn't followed through in the past.

"I should probably go mingle more," Andrew said as they saw someone coming their way. "It was nice talking to you, Kate."

They stayed for another twenty minutes or so and Kate was amused that Philippe seemed to know so many people there. Kristen had mentioned that she'd often seen him out at these kinds of events though. She recognized a few people herself, among them Violet Jones, the neighbor who had spoken out at the meeting to oppose The Beach Plum Cove Inn.

Violet was overdressed in Kate's opinion, although she did look gorgeous. She was wearing expensive black high heels, which Kate could see were the designer Louboutin, as the bottom of the shoe was famously red. Her dress was too, a bright, fire-engine red that was impossible to miss, especially with her tall, curvy figure. Her blonde hair cascaded down her back in a carefully arranged tumble of waves and her makeup was perfect. Her lipstick even matched her dress. Violet raised her eyes when she saw Kate. Philippe had gone to get them more champagne, and Kate was admiring one of the paintings, a watercolor of Nantucket harbor.

"Kate. I'm surprised to see you here!" Violet said.

"Really? Why is that?" Kate replied coolly.

"Well, I've just never seen you at these type of things before."

"I've been living in Boston. I've only been home for a few weeks."

"Oh, right. Sorry about that, I heard you lost your job." Violet sounded anything but sorry as Philippe returned and handed Kate a glass of champagne.

"Thank you. Philippe, do you know my mother's neighbor, Violet Jones?"

"No, I don't. It's nice to meet you." He held out his hand and Violet took it, holding it a moment longer than necessary.

"We have met actually. At an art show last Spring." Violet reminded him.

"Oh, that's right." Phillipe casually put his arm around Kate and pulled her close. "Now I know why your name sounds familiar. You spoke out against Kate's mother at the board of selectmen meeting."

Violet suddenly looked uncomfortable as she realized that Kate and Phillipe were together and that Phillipe was not likely to fall under her charms.

"If you'd both excuse me, I see someone I need to talk to. Have a great night."

Kate watched with amusement as Violet slithered off. Philippe relaxed his arm and took a step away.

"I don't care for her much," he said.

Kate laughed. "Well, that makes two of us. I don't

know why she was so against my mother's bed and break-fast proposal."

"I suspect she likes to be difficult."

They walked around a little more until they'd seen everything in the gallery and then said their goodbyes to Andrew and made their way to the Club Car for dinner.

WHEN THEY WALKED INTO THE CLUB CAR, THE hostess, a very pretty, younger woman with long dark hair and a perfect glowing complexion, came right over to them and gave Philippe a hug.

"How've you been? Your favorite table just opened up. I can take you right over."

Kate smiled. Apparently the Club Car was one of Philippe's favorite restaurants too.

"Great to see you again, Olivia. Do you know Kate Hodges?"

The younger woman smiled and looked as though she was trying hard to place Kate, but failed.

"I'm local, but just recently moved back to the island. It's nice to meet you," Kate said.

"You as well!" Olivia scooped up two menus and led them to a pretty corner table, with pale blue cushions and a white tabletop. It was a small restaurant, but not too crowded. Kate preferred to come in the off-season. During the summer, all the restaurants along the pier were packed, as tourists went there after getting off the ferries.

"Andrea will be right with you to get your drinks

order." Kate noticed a brief moment of hesitation flash across her face, but Olivia smiled as she walked off, so she didn't think anything of it. Until she saw a very pretty blonde girl walk their way and then stop short and go back into the kitchen. A minute later, a different waitress, with short, dark hair came to their table.

"Good evening, I'm Penny, and I'll be taking care of you tonight. Can I get you something to drink?"

Kate ordered a chardonnay and Philippe got a Dewar's and water.

"I thought Olivia said Andrea was going to be our server. I noticed another girl coming over here first, and then she went back into the kitchen. Isn't that strange?"

Philippe looked a bit uncomfortable. "I think that may be because of me. I was a regular here for a while, more so than I am now, and I dated a few of the waitresses. Andrea was one. She's a lovely girl, but she wanted to be a little more serious than I did."

Kate considered that as Penny returned with their drinks and set them down. She told them the specials for the night and then Philippe put in an order for the grilled local oysters with cilantro butter for the two of them to share. They both decided on the roasted cod with hazelnut romesco for their entrée. Penny took their menus and returned a few minutes later with a basket of hot bread and butter.

"Did you date Olivia too?" Kate asked. The hostess seemed unusually friendly and her eyes had lit up when she saw Philippe.

"No, she's a bit young for me." He paused and then added, "She does keep inviting me to her parties though.

We know a lot of the same people, and she does throw a good party."

Kate ripped a piece of bread in half and spread butter on it.

"What are you doing this weekend?" Philippe asked as he reached for the bread.

"Probably starting to move my things to my mother's friend's house. Why?"

"I have to go to L.A. For a few days. Why don't you come with me?"

"You want me to come with you to California? What would we do there?"

"Well, I have to meet with a few people at the studio, but that won't take long. We can take a ride up the coast, have dinner overlooking the ocean in Malibu or go to Spago in Hollywood for the best pizza you've ever had."

"And where would we stay?"

"I usually get a suite at the Four Seasons. The king sized bed is super comfy." He winked and Kate knew that many women would find his offer irresistible. She was tempted for about two seconds.

"You remind me a bit of my ex. We just recently broke up."

"Oh, how so?"

"He was a charmer. Too handsome for his own good and let's just say he loved women and enjoyed the attention."

Philippe grinned. "You think I'm charming? And handsome? That sounds like a good thing."

Kate laughed. "That's all you heard? Yes, you've obviously attractive. I think we may be looking for different things though." She hesitated for a moment, trying to find the right words. She really did like Philippe but not in the way that he wanted her to.

"I wasn't really looking to date anyone yet, but when I am, it will be someone who wants something more serious. I don't really do casual." She took a bite of bread and added, "But I would love to be friends. I really do enjoy your company. We have a lot in common, and aside from my sisters, I don't have many friends here. Most of the people I grew up with have moved off-island."

Philippe sighed and took Kate's hand and gave it a squeeze. "I think you're amazing. I wish I could tell you that I'm ready for something more serious, but I like you too much to lie to you." He grinned. "I'm not sure I ever will be, to be perfectly honest. I'm not in any hurry to settle down. I'm having too much fun. I have to travel quite a bit too, and that's hard on any relationship. It's just easier to keep things light."

Kate squeezed his hand back and let it go. She really liked him and was glad that he'd confirmed her suspicions.

Penny arrived with their grilled oysters and set them down in the middle of the table.

"You have to try one of these, they are incredible." Philippe reached for an oyster that was so hot the steam was coming off it. Kate took a moment to let it cool.

"I will." She smiled. "You know, I think that eventually, you're going to be shocked when you meet the right person and she knocks you off your feet. You won't want to date anyone else."

"I'm not so sure about that. But one never knows?"

Philippe looked skeptical, and Kate wondered if he might be right. After all, Dylan had sworn that he was a changed man. Kate decided to change the subject.

"So, I went to the library today, and did some research for my book. My next step will be making an outline. Does that take you very long?" She popped one of the grilled oysters in her mouth. The flavors were as good as Philippe had promised.

"It doesn't take me long at all. I don't outline."

Kate had assumed that she needed to make an extensive outline, to plan her book and where she needed to go.

"You don't? But how do you know what you need to write each day?"

He laughed. "I tried to outline once, and it sucked all the joy out of the story for me. But I know some people swear by it. You should definitely try it and see if it helps you. It's more fun for me to discover the story as I go."

"That sounds so much harder." Kate had always been a planner. She couldn't imagine just sitting down and staring at a blank page wondering what was supposed to happen.

"You have to dream up the story either way, whether it's for your outline or pantsing as we call it, when you just write and see where the story takes you."

"That sounds terrifying to me. Especially in a mystery where I have to set things up and drop clues. I'll try an outline first I think."

"Good idea. Do you want that last oyster?" Philippe was nice to offer, but Kate knew he was dying for it.

"No, you have it. I don't want to spoil my appetite."

"Thanks. Why don't you show me your outline when

you get it finished? I can let you know if the structure looks solid and if the story is compelling. That is one benefit of an outline, you can fix that kind of thing before you write the book."

Kate appreciated the offer. It was generous of him, especially considering that she'd told him she didn't want to be more than friends.

"If you don't mind, I will take you up on that offer."

CHAPTER 10

K risten had barely eaten in the past few days since she'd last seen Sean. He'd called the next day as if everything was fine and wanted to make plans to go out again. He'd been shocked and not happy when Kristen firmly told him that she was ending their relationship. It felt like the right decision, but it still felt awful, and she'd been grieving what she'd thought they had.

But finally, after three days of misery, not eating enough and sleeping too much, she woke Friday morning and felt almost as if the fog had lifted. She had more energy, and she was starving. And there was nothing in her house to eat. She wanted to make a giant omelet and wash it down with many cups of coffee and she was out of both eggs and coffee. So, she had a cup of tea to take the edge off, and then headed downtown to the supermarket to do some grocery shopping.

Since she was hungry, she ended up buying twice

what she normally would. She lugged the bags out to her jeep, tossed them in the back seat and climbed in to drive home. As she sat waiting to pull out of the parking lot onto Main street, her phone rang. She saw that it was Sean and let it go to voice mail. It immediately rang again and she saw that it was Kate and went to answer it, but when she picked up the phone, it slipped out of her hands. She swore and reached over to get the phone and took her eyes off the road for two seconds.

But it was two seconds too long. She lifted her foot off the gas slightly and her car rolled forward and into something. She looked up and swore again. She'd rolled into an old navy Mercedes that was waiting to turn into the parking lot. The driver stopped his car, jumped out and came around front to assess the damage. And then he came her way.

Kristen took a deep breath and got out of the car. It was totally her fault. There wasn't a lot of damage, but she'd tapped his front bumper and there was a big scrape that showed the car was once beige.

"I'm so sorry," she said.

"You hit me!" The man standing in front of her sounded frustrated, and she didn't blame him. He was also somewhat familiar looking and very attractive. She didn't think she'd ever seen him on the island before though.

"Were you texting?" he accused her.

"What? No! My phone rang, and I went to answer and dropped it. I really am sorry. I've never hit anyone before." The stress of the past few days and her growling stomach caught up with her and Kristen suddenly felt like she might burst into tears. "Let me get my insurance information for you." Her voice cracked as she went to turn back to her car. His voice stopped her.

"Hold on a second. I don't think it's really that bad. It's just a scrape. We might not need to get our insurance companies involved."

"Okay. I'll totally pay for any repairs though."

The driver nodded. "Why don't we exchange numbers? I'll have a guy I know look at it, and we'll go from there?" He pulled a business card out of his wallet and handed it to her. She glanced at the name, Andrew Everly. The owner of the new art gallery. She fished in her purse for one of her cards and handed it to him. She'd designed her cards herself, and they represented her style, with a swirl of pale, pretty watercolors in the background. He smiled as he looked it over.

"You're an artist. It's funny, but someone actually mentioned your name to me recently. I looked you up online and liked what I saw. I was planning to reach out to you."

Kate's jaw dropped. It was the last thing she expected to hear after hitting the man's car.

"Thank you. That means a lot to me. My sister Kate, was at your open house the other night. She was impressed."

He thought for a moment. "She was with Philippe Gaston, right?"

"She was."

Andrew tucked her card in his front pocket. "I'll be in

touch after I talk to my car guy. Maybe we can work out a barter arrangement. I'd love to include a painting or two of yours at the gallery, and we could just deduct the cost of the paint job when they sell. It shouldn't be too much. It looks like it will just be a touch up."

Kristen relaxed a little. That seemed reasonable enough, and it was another opportunity to show her work, which was always a good thing.

"I'd love that. Thank you. And again, I'm really sorry about your car."

He smiled. "It's just paint. We'll talk soon, Kristen."

"So, how do you feel about being a grandmother?" Sue asked as she and Lisa strolled along Main street. They'd just had a quick lunch at Oath Pizza, Lisa's favorite place for pizza on the island. They made it to order by the slice, adding whatever toppings you wanted and passing it through a high speed oven, so it was almost ready by the time you reached the cash register. They'd had two big slices each and decided to walk it off by window shopping.

Lisa found herself slowing down every time they passed a window that had anything baby related. She came to a full stop in front of a yarn shop where there was a display of the tiniest, cutest baby socks in both pink and blue.

"Well, I'm thinking of taking up knitting, so I can make socks like those. What does that tell you?" Lisa laughed. "I'm thrilled. It's still very early stage though, so of course I worry about Abby and the baby's health. She's under a lot of stress these days."

"She and Jeff haven't worked things out yet? I thought they'd be back together by now. With the holidays and all."

"I know. I hoped that she would too. But, I think it's more serious than I originally thought. Seems like something has been bothering her for a long time."

"Jeff must be over the moon about the baby though? He has a good reason to work on things now. Or has she still not told him yet?"

"She's waiting until she's three months along. She's hoping that they can work things out by then and it won't be because of the baby."

"I feel for her. My first three months with each kid were hell. It must be hard for her to go through that alone." Sue had three children all grown, but none were married yet.

"I know. She has her up and down days. And we've seen more of her than we used to. The girls and I are trying to support her as much as possible. They're all coming over for dinner tonight actually."

"You're lucky that they all live here." Sue's children all lived off-island in different Boston suburbs.

"I know. I didn't think Kate would ever come back though. It's nice having her here, though I'm not sure how long it will last."

"You think she'll go back to Boston?"

"There's a good chance that she'll have to. Either

Boston or New York area, as that's where most of the media jobs are. Unless she can get enough freelance work."

"She's working on a book too, I think you mentioned?"

Kate smiled. "She is. A murder mystery. I can't wait to read it. But, from what I understand, it's very difficult to get published, so earning a living from books is a long shot. It would be marvelous though. I'm keeping my fingers crossed for her."

Sue looked thoughtful. "Maybe she could self-publish. Be an indie author. "

Lisa was surprised by the suggestion. "Really? I don't know much about that, but I always thought self-publishing was a last resort type of thing?"

"It used to be, but it's all the rage right now, thanks to Amazon and Apple. I just read something about it recently in the New York Times. And I've discovered some really good new authors this past year that are self-published. A few of them used to be with big publishers and do it themselves now."

"How interesting. I'll mention it to Kate. I'll be curious to hear what she thinks and what her plans are for the book once she finishes it." She was quiet for a moment before adding, "She's moving into Paige's place tomorrow. I'm going to miss having her home."

Sue chuckled. "Well, she won't be far away. She could walk over to visit you if she wanted to."

"I know. Or I could walk there. I could use the exercise."

"If she's moving out now does that mean you have all of your rooms rented? Already?"

Lisa nodded. "Yes. Kate posted some information online and we've had a steady stream of inquiries ever since. I have a couple coming in from London tomorrow evening, and this weekend three couples are coming to celebrate a thirtieth anniversary."

"Oh, how nice! You'll have a full house. How's Rhett?"

"He's great. He showed me around the restaurant the other day, and it looks like it's going to be really nice. I'm excited for it to open."

Sue looked intrigued. "So, you're spending a little bit of time with him? He's a good-looking man."

Lisa smiled. "We've become friends. I enjoy his company. I have breakfast with him most mornings, and he joined me for dinner the other night. I thought Kate was going to be there too, so it's not like it was a date or anything like that."

Lisa had worried that it might be awkward without Kate there that evening, but it hadn't been. She'd had a lovely time sharing her beef stew supper with Rhett. They'd laughed and talked for several hours after they finished eating and the time had flown by.

"But Kate wasn't there?" Sue said.

"No. She had a date with that writer, Philippe something."

"Gaston? The gorgeous French guy?"

"That's the one. I don't think they're dating anymore though."

"Oh, that's too bad."

"No, I think it's actually a very good thing. Kate needs someone more down to earth. She says she's not looking to date anyone for a while. I don't blame her. It must be hard to bounce right back after ending a two-year relationship."

"Well, they say you always find someone when you're not looking. Though, I'm not sure if that's true or not." Sue looked back at yarn shop. "Do you want to go inside?"

"Sure. Maybe I will get some yarn. I really wouldn't mind learning how to knit. Do you know how?"

Sue laughed at the idea of it. "Me? No. I'd be willing to learn with you though. Maybe we could take a class or something."

When they stepped inside, Lisa marveled at the array of yarn choices and colors. The owner of the shop, Beverly Campbell, was a lovely older woman that Lisa had seen around town for many years. Her eyes lit up when Sue asked if she had any beginner classes.

"We have a new session starting up this coming Monday night if you ladies are interested. We meet here from six to eight. The lessons run for four weeks and then you can transition into the knitting club if you like. That's on Tuesday evenings and it's a nice group of ladies of all skill levels."

"Those baby socks in the window. Will I learn enough to be able to knit a pair of those?" Lisa asked.

Beverly smiled. "Of course. And that's a perfect project to start with. Shall we pick out some yarn and needles for you both?"

Lisa and Sue exchanged glances and Sue nodded.

"Let's do it," Lisa said.

"SEAN ISN'T USED TO THE WORD NO," KRISTEN SAID. She dipped a chip in the lemony white bean hummus her mother had just set on the kitchen island and took a quick bite before continuing her story. Kate, Abby and her mother were all gathered in the kitchen for dinner.

"He's still trying to get you to change your mind? I never liked him much."

"I know, Mom. And I think you mentioned that the first week I met him. I should have listened then." She sighed. "I haven't been taking his calls, so he's been leaving long messages with all kinds of promises."

"What kind of promises?" Kate asked. Kristen could tell from her tone and expression that she shared their mother's opinion of Sean.

"Nothing I haven't heard before. The latest is that he wants to take me to Manhattan for a romantic getaway weekend so we can 'find each other' again."

Abby laughed. "I'm sorry, but that is so lame. He doesn't get it at all does he?"

Kristen nodded sadly. "No, he doesn't. He thinks that spending money on fancy dinners and hotels will win me back. None of his messages mention a thing about moving forward with his divorce."

"Maybe you should call him back and tell him to stop calling," Kate suggested gently.

Kristen felt a pit in her stomach at the thought of it, but she knew her sister was right.

"I'll do it tomorrow."

"Have you started writing your book, Kate?" Kristen asked. She was eager to change the subject.

"Sort of. I'm working on the outline and I'm almost done with it. Philippe said he'd take a look at it for me, to make sure it looks on track before I start the actual writing. But, I've already written most of the first two chapters, and that helped me to figure out the feel of the story. They'll probably change depending on his feedback."

"That's nice of him," their mother said. "I was chatting with Sue today, and she mentioned something about self-publishing and that it might be a good idea for you. Have you thought about that at all?"

Kate nodded. "I have actually. The traditional publishing process takes so long, getting an agent and submitting to publishers and waiting to hear back. And then if you get accepted it's often a year or longer before your book is out there. I thought I might publish this first one myself and see if I can build a reader base. Then maybe consider traditional publishing too, down the road."

"How does that work? Wouldn't you be better off with a regular publisher?" Kristen asked.

"Maybe. It's hard to say. I'm hearing from other writer friends that publisher advances are smaller than they've ever been before. And that you can earn more money, sometimes a lot more money by doing it yourself."

"But you'd have to do everything, get it edited, have a cover made, market it." It sounded horrible to Kristen. She hated the business side of making art.

But Kate laughed. "I actually like a lot of that stuff,

and I've learned about Facebook ads a bit at the magazine. Plus, I know a talented artist…maybe she could help me make a memorable cover?"

"Oh! That could actually be really cool." Kristen's mind immediately began to whirl as she pictured various images she could create.

"I haven't decided on anything for sure though. I still need to finish the book, make sure it works and see what Philippe says. I trust his judgment and am grateful he offered to help."

"Do you think he'll still be willing to help if you're not dating him?" Abby sounded cynical.

"I think he will. He seemed sincere. I really like him and I think we'll be good friends. I kind of think of him like a wayward brother."

"Speaking of brothers, is Chase dating anyone? He hasn't mentioned any girls lately," Kristen asked.

"I saw him talking to Lauren Snyder for quite a while the other night at the Chicken Box," Abby said.

Everyone turned to look at Abby in surprise.

"What were you doing at the Chicken Box?" Kate asked. It was one of the busiest bars on the island with live music and a younger crowd.

"Emily dragged me there. She wanted to go hear the band, and she thought it would do me good to get out." Emily was Abby's best friend and was very much single.

"And did it? Did you have fun?" Kristen asked.

Abby smiled. "I did actually. The band was really good, and the place wasn't too packed like it gets in the summer. Chase sat at the bar with Lauren for a long time. They looked deep in conversation so I didn't want to interrupt. I went to the bathroom and when I came out they were both gone, so I didn't get a chance to talk to him."

"Hmm, that's interesting. He hasn't mentioned her," Kate said.

"Didn't he date her a million years ago? In high school?" Kristen asked.

Abby laughed. "If you can call it that. They 'went out' for a week or two, but never really saw each other outside of school. One of the basketball players asked her to a dance, and she dropped Chase the same day. He was crushed."

"Does she live here year round? I can't picture her," Kate asked.

Abby reached for a chip. "She's pretty. Has really long, blonde hair that always looks like she just had it blown straight, but it's naturally like that. She lives here year round. After college, she worked in real estate in Boston and then moved home a few years later, and opened an office here with her brother. I only know because he's a friend of Jeff's."

"That seems risky," their mother said.

Abby nodded. "It was actually really smart. Her brother worked for one of the local builders all through school, so he knows a ton of people on the island. Lauren has Boston area connections—people that might be looking to buy or rent on Nantucket. Their office is doing really well."

"She doesn't sound like his usual type." Their mother didn't sound overly enthused about Lauren. And she was right. So far, Chase had mostly dated sweet girls that just wanted to have fun. He'd never been serious about any of them. And Lauren was unlike any girl he'd dated before. Kristen didn't like that she'd already broken his heart once.

"Maybe they were just catching up, or talking business. They probably know a lot of the same people," Abby said.

"Well, he hasn't mentioned her, so hopefully that's all it is." Their mother said. "I hope you girls are hungry? Dinner is ready. Help yourselves." She set a bubbling tray of lasagna in the middle of the table and stuck a serving spoon in it.

"I'm starving. But that seems to be a constant thing lately." Abby laughed as she scooped a huge piece of lasagna onto her plate.

While they ate, Kristen told them about her adventure in the parking lot. She noticed that Kate seemed especially interested when she mentioned who it was that she hit.

"I was hoping you'd get a chance to meet him soon, although this isn't quite what I had in mind. But it sounds like he was decent about it?"

Kristen nodded. "He was. I'm happy to give him a few paintings to put in the gallery." She knew which two she wanted to give him. Two of her most recent that she was especially excited about. She was curious to see how they'd do.

"When do you move into Paige's house?" Kristen asked her sister.

"Tomorrow." Kate reached for a second slice of garlic bread.

"Do you need help to move your stuff over there?"

Kate laughed. "No, thank you though. I don't have much here to move. If you want to stop over to visit later, I should be all settled by end of the day."

"I'll do that."

CHAPTER 11

L isa was enjoying her morning coffee as she sat at the kitchen island reading the local newspaper. She turned at the sound of footsteps coming down the stairs. Kate was lugging her one big suitcase and an overnight bag. Lisa set her coffee cup down and walked over to her daughter.

"I feel awful that you have to move out. If you want to stay, you could sleep on the living room sofa for a few nights. After the three couples leave, I'm not fully booked." Lisa felt guilty that her daughter was moving out, and she was going to miss having her around. The house had felt livelier since she'd been home.

Kate set her luggage down in the hallway and gave her mother a hug.

"Don't be silly. I'll be right up the road, and it looks like I'll be on the island at least through the winter, so you'll probably be sick of seeing me, anyway." She grinned as she picked up her overnight bag and grabbed the handle of her suitcase. She didn't seem to mind that she'd been kicked out. Lisa knew she'd probably love staying at Paige's place. It was beautifully decorated with gorgeous water views and was the perfect size for a single person.

"All right, honey. I'll see you soon then."

"I'll come by Saturday morning to help with breakfast, and to check out your new guests." Kate promised as she walked out the door.

The house immediately felt empty without Kate in it. Lisa sighed as she topped off her coffee and settled back into her spot at the island. She was as curious as Kate about their new guests. She hoped that they'd be pleased with the accommodations. She'd made sure there would be fresh flowers in all the rooms and extra towels in the bathrooms. She'd tried to anticipate all the things a guest might appreciate.

She smiled as she thought of Rhett. They'd quickly become good friends, and she'd been enjoying his company for the occasional evening meal. She hoped that the arrival of the guests wouldn't be too distracting for him. He'd had the upstairs of the house to himself so far.

LESS THAN TEN MINUTES LATER, KATE PULLED INTO THE driveway of Paige's house. She'd always admired it and was looking forward to staying there for the next few months. She fished the key out of her pocket and unlocked the front door, then went back to get her luggage and brought everything inside.

Once she was in, she took a moment to look around.

Big picture windows in the living/family room looked out over the ocean and the sweeping views of the bay were breathtaking. The kitchen had creamy ivory painted cabinets and a v-shaped rose colored granite island that faced the living room.

Kate knew that Paige wasn't much of a cook, but the kitchen was still a chef's dream. It had a six-burner gas stove in the center of the island, so someone could cook while enjoying the view and chatting with guests sitting across from them.

The house was much smaller than her mother's. But it still had plenty of room, with three bedrooms. Paige used one of them as an office and Kate planned to do the same. She brought her luggage into the master bedroom which was roomy and full of light. The sun poured through French doors that led to a small balcony overlooking the ocean. It was too cold to sit out there now, but Kate could picture herself enjoying her morning coffee there in warmer weather.

She'd assumed that she would take the guest bedroom, but Paige had insisted that she stay in the bigger, main bedroom.

"My winter clothes are in storage now and I'm taking most of everything else with me, so you'll have plenty of room in the closet," she'd said.

Sure enough, there was more than enough room for Kate's clothes in the large, walk-in closet. She spent the next hour unpacking and putting everything away. And then she took her laptop into Paige's office, which was starkly empty compared to the rest of the house. There was a large, white desk, facing a bay window with pretty water views. The only thing on the desk was a roll of stamps and a small reading lamp.

Kate set her laptop down, plugged it in and opened up her mystery project. She had it fully outlined now and the first two chapters done and sent off to Philippe for feedback. He'd volunteered to read and make sure she was on the right track. He'd also called the day before to say he'd come by tonight to give her feedback in person. She'd thought he'd do it by email and she hated to bother him, but he'd insisted.

"All my notes are handwritten. That's how I read. I print it out and make notes in the margins," he'd said.

"Well, why don't you plan to come for dinner then? Do you like meatballs and pasta?" Kate figured she could make a big pot of sauce and let it simmer while she worked.

"Who doesn't? I'll bring the wine." He sounded so enthusiastic, and she was eager to hear his feedback. She knew her idea was a good one, but she was less sure if the story was working the way she'd laid it out. She hoped so.

After staring out the window for at least twenty minutes as she thought about the story, she finally started writing. She wrote for several hours before her shoulders and neck began to protest and her stomach told her it was time to break for lunch. She knew there wasn't any food in the house and she had to pick up the ingredients for dinner anyway, so she took a ride into town to Stop and Shop, the island's biggest market.

An hour later, she returned home with several bags of groceries, made herself a quick turkey sandwich and threw the meatballs and sauce together. She baked the meatballs first and then added them to the big pot of sauce that was simmering on the stove. Once that was set, she returned to the office to dive into her story. She was eager to get back to it. She'd been a little unsure of what needed to happen next when she stopped for lunch. But the perfect solution came to her as she was driving home from the market, and she wanted to get it down before it slipped away.

The afternoon flew by as Kate lost herself in her story. Her new idea was a good one, and she was surprised when she finally stopped for the day, to see how much she'd done. The sun was beginning to set as she yawned and stretched. The smell of simmering tomato sauce tickled her nose, and she went to the kitchen to check on dinner. She'd left the heat on low and the sauce was bubbling happily. She dipped a teaspoon in for a quick taste. All it needed was a pinch of salt and pepper.

She still had an hour or so before Philippe was due to arrive. A hot shower revived and soothed her achy shoulders and arms that were stiff from sitting in the same position for too long. After blowing her hair dry, she dressed in her favorite worn jeans and a baby blue V-neck sweater. She set a pan of water on the stove to boil for the pasta, and just as it started to boil, she was surprised by a knock on the door. Philippe didn't strike her as the type to arrive so early.

She was even more surprised when she opened the door to find Jack Trattel standing there. He looked as though he'd just come home from work as he was wearing jeans and a navy blue heavy work shirt with Trattel Seafood embroidered in red across the front.

"Hi Jack."

He grinned. "I saw a car in the driveway and thought it might be you. I remembered you said you were going to be staying here for a while."

"Good memory. Do you want to come in?" She opened the door wider, and he stepped inside.

"Sure. Just for a minute though. I don't want to keep you." He followed her to the kitchen and stopped short when saw the pot of simmering sauce.

"Something smells good."

"Thanks. It's just spaghetti and meatballs," she said as she emptied a box of pasta into the pot of boiling water.

"That's a lot of pasta. If you need any help to eat it, let me know." He grinned again and Kate laughed. He looked starving.

"Why don't you join us? I'm sure Philippe won't mind."

At the mention of his friend's name, Jack's eyes clouded. "I didn't realize you were expecting company." A moment later, he added, "I'm just teasing, anyway. I told my brother that I'd meet him in about an hour for pizza and beers."

"That sounds fun too."

"Yeah. Well, I should probably get going. I just wanted to welcome you to the neighborhood." He stepped toward the front door and Kate followed.

"Well, thanks for stopping by. Which house is yours?"

"The gray one two doors down. We're almost next-door neighbors. If you need anything, just holler. I'll probably hear you."

Kate hadn't realized that he lived that close. She'd

known he was on the same street.

Jack stepped outside as Philippe pulled into the driveway.

"I'll talk to you later. Enjoy your date night."

Kate opened her mouth to say it wasn't a date night, but Jack was already gone and saying hello to Philippe as he got out of his car. She couldn't hear the two of them but a moment later, they both laughed and Jack got into his car and drove off.

Kate held the door open for Philippe who was smiling and carrying a bag with two bottles of wine sticking out of it, and something else that she couldn't quite make out.

"Hello, beautiful." Philippe leaned in and kissed her lightly on the cheek.

He handed her the bag which she brought into the kitchen and set on the counter. He'd brought two bottles of a good Amarone, one of Kate's favorite red Italian wines. And a gorgeous small bouquet of pink tulips in a square cut vase.

"These are lovely. Thank you!" She set the flowers in the middle of the island. She figured they'd eat there. When she turned back, Philippe had found the wine opener and was opening one of the bottles. She got two wine glasses from the cupboard. He poured them each a glass and handed one to her.

She took a small sip and sighed. The wine was wonderful, smooth and full-bodied.

"This is really good. Thank you."

Philippe smiled and lifted his glass. "To a future best-selling author!" He tapped his glass against hers and she laughed, loving his enthusiasm. She also felt a bit of relief.

"Does that mean you didn't hate my pages? I have to confess, I was worried about what you'd think," she admitted.

"Of course I didn't hate them. They're actually quite good, better than I expected. There's a few things here and there that I'll point out, but they're minor fixes. You have a solid premise. I'm looking forward to reading more."

"You are? Really?" Kate was floored. She'd felt like she was imposing as it was.

"Really. When you finish your first draft, send it along. I'll read and give you some big picture feedback. You're on the right track though."

"That's incredibly generous of you. I'll gladly take you up on it. And I'll owe you another dinner."

"I look forward to it."

When the pasta was done, Kate drained it, then filled two plates with pasta, meatballs and sauce. She also set out parmesan cheese, bread and butter. They settled at the island and dove in. Philippe was impressed with the meatballs.

"These are amazing, as good as any I've had in a restaurant."

Kate laughed. "Thank you. It's one of the few things I know how to make well."

They both went back for a second helping and then finished off one of the bottles of wine as they sat talking for well over an hour. Philippe had some great suggestions for her story which she knew would make it tighter and stronger. When they finished going over the feedback, he made her laugh telling her about his upcoming TV project and the crazy cast of characters that were involved.

"Filming starts in two weeks, and I won't be around as much for a few months until the season wraps. I might get home a few weekends a month, hopefully."

"Would it be easier to just live there full-time?" she wondered.

"Oh, much easier in some ways. But, I'd miss the island too much. This is what I consider home. As soon as I step off the plane and breathe in the Nantucket air, it's like all the stress leaves my body. It's kind of hard to explain."

"No, I get it. That's exactly how I feel too, though I'm usually arriving by ferry."

"Do you think you'll stay here? Or move back to Boston?"

"I'm really not sure. It depends how things go this winter and if I'm able to get enough freelance work to allow me to stay. There are more jobs in Boston."

Philippe frowned at the thought.

"If the rest of your book is as good as your first chapters, hopefully you won't have to worry about that." His words gave her hope and made her feel excited to make his changes and continue with the story.

"Do you ever doubt that what you've written is good enough?" she asked. She was sure if he did, it was a long time ago, but still she was curious.

He smiled. "Yes, all the time. With every book actually." His answer surprised her.

"Really? Still?"

"From what I hear, it's normal. Most writers feel that

way at some point in their process. So you're in good company. Just keep going."

"I will," she promised.

"Well, I should probably get going. Unless you want to open that other bottle of wine? But then I might be here longer than you'd like. And I might forget about our agreement to just be friends?" He grinned, and she couldn't help but laugh. He was like a mischievous child at times. A very good-looking, charming one to be sure. And she knew that more wine would be a very bad idea.

"I think I've had my limit. And we both have to work tomorrow I think?" She wasn't sure if he was or not, but she didn't want to be feeling hung-over in the morning.

He stood. "Well, it was worth a shot, right? I'll give you a call when I'm back on the island, and we'll see how far along you are then."

"That sounds, good. Thanks again for all of your help and for the wine, and flowers."

"It was my pleasure, all of it." Philippe wrapped her in a hug and kissed her cheek again before walking out the door.

Once he left, all the energy seemed to leave the room. Kate wondered if she'd done the right thing to discourage his interest. He'd been such good company, making her laugh all night and taking a sincere interest in her book. She appreciated that he cared. And he was certainly handsome, she definitely found him attractive. But there was still a little voice that seemed to whisper, "He's not for you." She'd learned in the past that it was usually a good idea to listen to that voice.

CHAPTER 12

Kristen had been sitting cross-legged on the floor of her studio for hours. The light was gorgeous all day, and the time had flown by. When the light changed, she started to notice her muscles growing stiff and an uncomfortable gnawing in her stomach. She hadn't eaten since early morning. She yawned and stretched and assessed her work. And then she smiled. It had been a good day. Her latest painting was done, and she felt goose bumps as she looked at it. Now and then, what she envisioned matched what ended up on canvas, and it was both thrilling, and deeply satisfying.

She stood and went to the bathroom to wash her hands. And laughed when she saw her reflection in the mirror. She looked a fright. Her hair was in a tangled, messy ponytail and she had a smudge of blue paint on her cheek. She scrubbed it off and was debating between jumping in the shower and eating something, anything, when she heard a knock at the door.

She ignored it for a moment, wondering who it could

be. The only people who would drop by were her sisters, and Sean but it was rare for any of them. Given how her last conversation with Sean went, she doubted it was him. It was probably Kate, and Kristen was sure if she checked her phone, which was charging in the bedroom, that she probably had a few missed calls. Maybe Kate would want to go grab a bite to eat. Kristen felt ready to celebrate the finishing of her painting, and she was starving with no food in the house.

She opened the door with a smile that faded as soon as she saw Andrew from the art gallery, standing on her doorstep. She hated that he was seeing her looking such a mess and was equally irritated that he hadn't called first.

"I'm sorry to just drop by. I called several times first, but you didn't answer. I was in the area and thought I'd try. Maybe you didn't get the messages? I'm not usually so rude." He looked as though he was regretting his impulse, and Kristen guessed her irritation was evident. She'd been told that her face was an open book. He looked so uncomfortable that she softened, her irritation faded, and she felt bad for him.

"It's all right. I didn't get any calls today. I've been working and had my phone charging in another room."

He looked ever more uncomfortable. "I'm so sorry. I didn't mean to interrupt your work. I'll let you get back to it, we can set a time for another day. Or I can just call again, whatever is easiest."

Kristen opened her door wide. "Come on in. I'm done for the day. You just caught me actually. I was debating whether to get in the shower or make something to eat, but the shower was winning."

He laughed. "I promise I won't keep you long. I met with my car guy, and he said the damage is really minimal, just a few hundred dollars."

Kristen looked around for her purse. "I can write you a check now."

"No, no, that's not what I'm suggesting. I was serious when I said I'd like to feature a couple of your paintings."

"Oh, okay. And you'll be sure to deduct the money out of my commission then?"

He hesitated for just a second. "Yes, of course. Did you have any paintings in mind? If you have anything ready, that is."

"I have a few in mind. But I just finished one today, that you might want to consider. It turned out pretty well." She wasn't one to brag, but she was excited by her newest painting and eager for him to see it. It felt like her best work yet.

A look came into his eyes, curiosity and a keen interest. "I'd love to see it. To see anything you have that's ready."

Kristen laughed. "I have a whole room of paintings. Follow me."

She led him into her studio and first took him into a side room where she kept her completed works. At least twenty paintings lined the walls. She let him look around and pointed out the two that she had in mind. He nodded in appreciation. "Those are lovely. I'd happily take any of these though. You're amazing." He sounded so sincere that Kirsten felt herself blush a little. She never had gotten used to receiving compliments.

They went into the studio, to where the newly finished

painting sat on its easel. Andrew stopped short and stared silently. He didn't speak for several long moments.

"Wow. That's simply gorgeous. You just finished it today?"

She nodded. "The light was perfect. I didn't expect to finish today, but it came together."

"It certainly did. I can have this one too?" He sounded like he was worried she might change his mind.

"Yes, and the other two as well, if you want them."

"I want them. But this one, is really special." He stared at it for another long moment and she wondered what he was thinking. He finally turned and told her. "I'd like to do a solo show for you with a few additional paintings if you're amenable to that?" He was all business now, and Kristen was thrilled that he wanted to give her a show of her own.

"Of course. Pick out whichever ones you'd like." They walked back into the room, and Andrew was like a kid in a candy store, as he looked around the room again. It was clear that he loved most of them and was having a hard time deciding. Finally, he settled on three more, and she saw that he was going for an ocean theme. All the paintings he chose featured the ocean and beach in some way.

They picked a date for the show that was several weeks out.

"I'll stop by a few days before to collect the paintings."

"I'll have them ready and wrapped for you."

Her stomach rumbled loudly and Kristen wanted to die of embarrassment.

"Sorry about that. I tend to forget to eat while I'm working."

"I was actually on my way to get a burger at Flynn's. Do you want to join me? If you don't already have plans that is. And it's the least I can do for barging in on you like his." He grinned. "I could talk about art for hours. And I'd love to learn more about you and how you became the artist that you are."

His enthusiasm was contagious and it would be fun to talk about art with someone who really understood her passion. Kristen was feeling antsy and on a high after finishing her painting. And she had a feeling that she'd enjoy his company.

"I'd love to. But I need a quick shower first. If you don't mind waiting. I won't be long."

"Of course I don't mind. I have some calls I need to make, so take your time."

Kristen grabbed some clothes and towels and headed into the bathroom. The hot water felt wonderful, and she wished she could stay in longer, letting it wash over her. But, she didn't want to be rude and keep Andrew waiting too long. Ten minutes later, she was done and changed into jeans and a flattering turquoise blue top. She dried her hair quickly, brushed her teeth and then she was ready.

When she came out of the bathroom, Andrew was just finishing a call. He smiled when he saw her. She grabbed her purse from the kitchen counter.

"I'm ready."

Andrew insisted on driving, saying it was silly for them both to drive when Flynn's was barely five minutes away.

She climbed into his car, cringing for a moment when she saw the deep scratch on the side again. He saw her look.

"My guy assured me it's really nothing. It's going to be fixed next Tuesday. Don't give it another thought."

And she didn't. For the next two hours, over messy burgers and fries and a couple of beers, Kristen had the best time she'd had in ages. Andrew was easy to talk to. They were both animated in their conversation, almost like when friends haven't seen each other in a while and have so much to catch up on. They liked a lot of the same artists and disagreed on others. And they knew a lot of the same people.

"It's surprising that we haven't run into each other before this," Andrew said at one point.

"I don't really go out all that much. I go through stretches where I'm quite the hermit, actually. I like to go out, but with smaller groups. Big parties sap my energy."

He nodded. "My twin sister is like that. We're alike in a lot of ways, she loves the arts too. She's a musician, a singer-songwriter. But she gets terrible stage fright."

"Would I know of her?" Kristen wondered. She was intrigued that he had a twin sister.

He grinned. "You might. Cassie Everly."

Kristen's jaw dropped. Andrew's sister was huge. One of the biggest folk artists in the country and recently released a record that was climbing the charts. She'd just been humming along to her newest single as she drove into town the day before. It was getting a lot of airplay on the radio.

"That's impressive. I love her music, and I can't believe she still gets nervous to go on stage."

"Cassie loves to perform once she gets going, but she needs to recharge after. I'm the opposite."

"You are?"

"I get my energy from being around people. And I love a good party. That's why my job suits me so well. I get to surround myself with art-lovers, hold shows, go to art events, or any gathering really. It's all good."

"I always enjoy an art show, though I prefer when it's someone else's show. It's more relaxing. I don't love being the center of attention," she admitted.

She saw understanding in his eyes. "I'll be right there with you when we do the show. And the champagne will be flowing. That might help a little."

She laughed. "Yes, it will actually, and I do love champagne. Plus I'm sure my sisters will come. It's great having both of them here now."

"I'm excited to do a show for you. I was thinking of Daffodil weekend, if that works for you? A lot of my New York friends said they'd be coming that weekend. Plus, it will be busy anyway."

"It's a crazy weekend. Every year it's busier than the year before as more people hear about it. That weekend would be fine with me. Better than fine, actually. I appreciate it." Having a show that weekend was huge. It would be a wonderful chance for her work to be exposed to a wider audience than usual.

"It will be fun. Oh, and I'd like to set up an auction for your new painting with a minimum starting bid." He mentioned an initial price that was more than twice what Kristen had ever sold a painting for. The thought made her nervous. What if it was too much, and no one bid? She voiced the concern, and he chuckled.

"I'm actually tempted to start even higher, but I want as many people bidding as possible. It will drive the price even higher. Some of my friends can be competitive when they want the same thing."

Kristen thought he was crazy. But he was the expert.

"Trust me. It will work out fine," he assured her.

They split a piece of chocolate pecan pie for dessert, and Kristen was happily stuffed. It had been a long day and a surprisingly fun dinner. She enjoyed Andrew's company. He insisted on paying the bill and while he was signing the charge slip, she took a long look at him.

He was handsome, but what made him attractive was his easy smile and enthusiasm, especially when he was talking about his favorite subject, and hers. She felt as if they were old friends already. Their conversation had been that comfortable. And it was purely friendship that she wanted from him.

She didn't get the impression that he wanted more from her either. They were both just excited to have made a new friend. Kristen knew she wasn't open to more than that right now from anyone, even Andrew. Her heart was still hurting over Sean, and it surprised her. She'd thought she was fine with casual. She always used to be and preferred it. She wasn't sure about anything anymore, but knew that she needed some time to herself and with her sisters and friends, and now she counted Andrew as one of those friends.

They continued chatting easily during the short ride

home and when he pulled up in front of her house, she impulsively leaned over and hugged him.

"Thank you for stopping by. It was really great talking to you, and it was exactly what I needed. I just ended a relationship," she admitted. "It was a long time coming, but it was still hard, and I've been focusing all my energy on work. It was really nice to get out tonight and just relax. I need to do that more."

"You do. I fully support that." He grinned. "Seriously though. Anytime you want to hang out, grab a bite or just catch up over coffee, give me a shout. You have my number, right?"

She had his business card in her wallet, from the day she'd hit him. "I do."

"Well, we'll talk soon then. Have a good night, Kristen."

He waited until she was inside before he drove off. She smiled to herself as she locked her door behind her. It had been a pretty great day, and she knew that Andrew was going to be a good friend. She looked forward to visiting with him again and she was both excited and nervous about her upcoming show. She couldn't wait to tell her sisters and mother.

CHAPTER 13

"Daffodil weekend? That's fantastic honey. You couldn't have picked a better weekend." Lisa was thrilled for her daughter. Both Kristen and Kate had just arrived Saturday morning for breakfast. Kristen was animated as she told them about Andrew stopping by, their dinner at Flynn's and her upcoming show. Kate looked at her sister with interest.

"He's single you know. Did that come up in your conversation?"

"No. It's not like that. We're just friends. Good friends I think. I feel as if I've known him much longer. We were practically finishing each other's sentences." She smiled. "Plus, I told him that I just ended a relationship, and he knows I'm not looking for that with him, with anyone right now."

"Hmm. Some people might consider him a catch," Kate said.

Kristen looked uncomfortable. "He's a great guy. I'm just not ready to consider dating anyone yet."

"I don't blame you, honey. Take all the time you need. There's no need to rush," Lisa said. She couldn't help notice though that her daughter had never lit up that way when she'd talked about her ex, Sean. The family had never been keen on Sean though. Lisa had suspected that he had no intention of leaving his wife anytime soon, if ever, when Kristen started dating him. But, she didn't voice her concerns. Kristen needed to find her own way, even if Lisa was fairly sure that Sean had been telling her what she wanted to hear.

She'd actually seen him at Blackeyed Susan's recently when she was there for breakfast with Sue. Sean, his wife and son were all having breakfast and looked like a happy family. Lisa was glad that Kristen had finally ended things with him.

"So, what are the guests like?" Kristen tried to change the subject.

"They seem lovely. They're from Long Island, and it's their first time on Nantucket."

"What did you make them for breakfast?" Kate asked.

"My cinnamon walnut coffee cake, fresh fruit, cream cheese and bagels, and a lobster quiche."

"You made a coffee cake and lobster quiche? My two favorites. They're going to love it," Kate said.

Lisa hoped so. She'd been making the coffee cake for years. It was full of butter and sour cream and goodness. And the lobster quiche was decadent and heavenly. Fresh sweet lobster in silky, creamy custard. It was a newer recipe, but it wowed everyone.

"Rhett is in for a treat," Kristen said.

"It was his idea, actually. We were chatting at breakfast the other day, and he mentioned that he loves lobster. I already knew that he loves quiche." She was looking forward to seeing his reaction. So far, he claimed to love everything that she cooked. She wasn't sure if he was just easy to please or if he really was that much of a fan of her food. Either way, she was glad that he enjoyed it.

"It's almost eight. Do you girls want to help me carry everything in?" Lisa poured a pot of freshly brewed coffee into a big thermos so guests could help themselves and it would stay hot. Kate grabbed the quiche and Kristen the platter of ice topped with fresh cut fruit and cream cheese. The bagels were already in the dining room. Lisa followed with the coffee and a carafe of freshly squeezed orange juice.

"Help yourselves. We'll eat here with the guests. Rhett will probably be along any minute."

"Did someone say my name?" Lisa turned at the sound of the familiar, deep voice. Rhett stood in the doorway looking casually handsome in a Nantucket red sweatshirt and jeans. He poured himself a coffee. Lisa had learned that Rhett liked to ease into his morning. He always had a cup of coffee first and relaxed over the morning paper or chatted with Lisa and then went for a second cup and some food.

"You girls both know Rhett?" Lisa said. She knew Kate had met him, but wasn't as sure about Kristen.

"Nice to see you again," Kate said.

"I don't think we've met yet, I'm Kristen." She introduced herself and Rhett smiled.

"You're the artist. Your mother showed me some of your work. You're very talented."

Kristen looked surprised and pleased by the compliment. "Thank you."

"She's having a show at the new gallery downtown over Daffodil weekend," Lisa told him.

He looked impressed. "That should be a busy weekend. I'll try to stop by if I can. If all goes well, the restaurant will be opening that weekend too."

Kate joined them at the table and set down a plate with a slice of quiche and some fruit. "How is that going so far?" she asked.

"As well as can be expected. We've had a few delays, the wrong flooring was sent, but that was fixed quickly enough. I've been meeting with vendors this week. I want to make sure we're using the best providers. Only one I haven't decided on yet is seafood. Who do you go to, Shipley or Trattel?"

"Trattel." Lisa and Kate said at the same time, while Kristen yawned and added more sugar to her coffee. She wasn't much of a breakfast eater, never had been. Lisa knew that she often forgot to eat when she was busy. Of all her children, Kristen had always had the worst eating habits, and Lisa thought she was too thin. But she didn't want to be one of those mothers who encouraged her children to eat more. She knew Kristen was healthy enough.

"I went to school with Jack Trattel," Kate said. "It's a family business, and he seems to be running it now."

"I liked Jack. He came to see me yesterday and assured me that they can handle whatever size orders we might need. The Shipley guy seemed good too. Guess I can't go wrong either way. Since you know Trattel, I'll give them a shot first." He looked at Kate's plate of fluffy quiche and then at Lisa. "You really made lobster quiche?"

Lisa smiled. "I did."

"And it's amazing." Kate popped a bite in her mouth as Rhett got up to refill his coffee and make a plate.

"Did I hear someone say lobster quiche? Or are my ears playing tricks on me?" A woman about Lisa's age stood in the dining room doorway, and Lisa waved her in. Her husband followed right behind her.

"Welcome. And yes, there's freshly made lobster quiche, fruit, bagels and hot coffee. Help yourselves," Lisa said.

Once the couple joined them at the table, Lisa introduced everyone. "Jennifer and Ed Barnes, meet my daughters, Kristen and Kate and your neighbor, Rhett Byrne."

"Nice to meet you all. The others should be along shortly," Jennifer said. She took a bite of quiche and swooned. "I've never had anything like this. Could I possibly get the recipe? It's decadent."

Lisa laughed. "Of course. I'm glad you like it. I'll email it to you. It's a basic quiche recipe, the secret ingredient is just fresh lobster." She looked at Rhett. "I bought mine at Trattel's, freshly shucked."

"Well, that confirms my decision then. Trattel's it is. Looks like I'm going to need another walk on the beach."

"Do you have any suggestions for where we should go to dinner tonight?" Jennifer asked. "It's Stacy's fiftieth birthday, so we want to make it really special."

While Lisa was thinking about the different options,

Kate and Kristen both spoke at the same time. "Keeper's"

"It's really fabulous," Kate said.

"It's my favorite special occasion place," Kristen added.

"I haven't been there in ages, but the girls are right. It's really lovely."

Rhett smiled. "That would be my pick too, since my restaurant isn't open yet. But once we are, we hope to give Keeper's a run for its money."

"Oh, you're opening a restaurant? How exciting. When will it be open?" Jennifer asked.

While Rhett told her all about it, the other two couples strolled in, looking sleepy and in need of coffee. Lisa welcomed them and introduced them to the girls and Rhett. They seemed like nice people, close friends that wanted to make a fiftieth birthday extra special.

"We're going sight-seeing today. Is there anything special we shouldn't miss?" Stacy asked.

"There's a wonderful whaling museum right downtown. Lots of great history, and you could walk around before or after and explore some of the shops. If you like art, there are galleries and little shops along the pier and if you want something quick and casual for lunch, there are lots of takeout places," Kristen said.

"That sounds fun. We'll get a bit of exercise walking around too," Jennifer said.

"If you want to do something a little different, there are walking ghost tours at night. They walk along downtown and stop at different houses telling the ghost story that goes along with it. Nantucket is supposedly very haunted," Kate said with a grin.

"That sounds better than shopping," Ed said.

"There are deep sea fishing trips too. I'm not sure what's running this time of year, but there's probably something," Lisa suggested.

"I'd like to look into that," Stacy's husband, Paul said.

"Well, we have the whole weekend, so we can look into everything and make a plan," Jennifer said.

Once all the guests except Rhett were finished eating and left to enjoy the day, the girls brought the leftover food into the kitchen. Rhett lingered over coffee and was the last to leave. Once the girls were out of the room, he stood.

"Well, I'm off for that walk. I'd invite you to join me, but you have more important company this morning. I hope we're still on for dinner tonight?"

"Yes, I'm looking forward to it." Rhett had suggested dinner the day before, and it would be the first time they went out to one of the local restaurants.

"Good. I'll come for you a little past six, and we'll set out. You pick the restaurant."

He set off for his walk, and Lisa brought the nearly empty coffee thermos and carafe of juice into the kitchen. Kate was putting the leftover quiche into a smaller bowl, while Kristen was nibbling on a piece of fruit.

"Rhett seems really nice. And single?" Kristen asked.

Lisa knew what she was suggesting. "He is single and yes, very nice. We're actually going out to dinner tonight."

That got Kate's interest. "You're dating him now?"

Was she? "I'm not sure it's actually a date. We're friends. I enjoy his company."

"Sounds like a date to me." Kristen smiled. "I'm all for it. We might have to come for breakfast again tomorrow to hear how it went."

Lisa laughed. "You're both welcome for breakfast anytime, but I don't expect there will be much to report. It's just dinner."

THOUGH SHE HAD TOLD THE GIRLS THAT HER DINNER plans with Rhett wasn't a date, Lisa was having an unusually hard time deciding what to wear for her 'non-date'. And she was feeling a little jittery, which seemed silly. She tried to focus on the two options she'd laid out on her bed, both of which were perfectly fine. She tried on both, twirled in front of her mirror and went with the dark navy blue sweater dress. It had a flattering neckline and hid the extra pounds that always crept up over the holidays.

She paired it with her favorite pearl necklace and drop earrings. She curled her hair just a hint, so that it fell in soft waves to her shoulders and she added a bit of blush to her cheeks. A swipe of berry-colored lipstick and a little black mascara and she was as ready as she was ever going to be.

When she heard the knock on her door, Lisa was surprised and a bit annoyed by the butterflies that started dancing in her stomach. Rhett was right on time. She took a deep breath and let him in.

"You look beautiful." His smile reached his eyes and sent a spray of laugh lines around his mouth and eyes. They made him even more attractive.

"Thank you. You're looking very handsome yourself." His wavy dark brown hair looked as though he'd had a trim earlier in the day. He was wearing a Nantucket red button-down shirt with tan pants and a chocolate brown tweed blazer.

"Have you decided where you'd like to go?"

"Well, we could go downtown. The Club Car, Center Street Bistro or Keeper's are always good. Depends what you are in the mood for."

"Want to give Keeper's a go? See if it's still as good as I remember?"

"Sure. It's one of my favorites, actually. But I haven't been in ages." The last time was with Brian. They'd run up a bigger than usual bill—Brian ordered an expensive bottle of wine and appetizers before dinner. Looking back, she realized it was after one of his rare casino trips, when he'd won instead of lost.

When they arrived at the restaurant, it was busy, but the woman at the front desk told them that it shouldn't be too long of a wait for a table for two. There were a few open seats at the small bar, so they settled in to wait. Rhett ordered drinks for them both, a glass of chardonnay for Lisa and a Jack and Coke for himself.

"Would you like to see menus? Or are you waiting for a table?" The bartender asked as she set their drinks in front of them. She'd introduced herself as Sami. She looked vaguely familiar and Lisa guessed that she was around Chase and Abby's age.

"We were going to wait for a table." Rhett looked at Lisa. "Unless you'd like to eat here?"

She looked around the room, where every table was taken. The bar was actually quite cozy. It was shaped like a semi-circle with only six seats. It was comfortable enough, and Lisa was suddenly very hungry.

"I'm fine eating here."

"I guess we'll take those menus." Sami handed them each a menu and said that the nightly specials were baked scallops and prime rib. After a careful study of the menu, they both went with the specials. Scallops for Lisa and prime rib for Rhett.

They chatted easily as they ate. Rhett gave her the latest update on how the restaurant was coming along. Every day seemed to bring a new drama.

"So, the woman I hired to oversee the waitstaff came highly recommended, but she told me this morning that she's had a change of heart and is moving to Bali."

"Bali!" Lisa couldn't help but laugh, even though she sympathized with his predicament.

"I know. If it happened to someone else, it would be so much funnier. You really can't make this stuff up. The good news, though is that she found me a replacement. Her sister is interested."

"Oh, well that's good, right? As long as she doesn't get the urge to go to Bali too."

Rhett smiled. "She's married with two little kids. I don't think she's going anywhere. She's home with the kids during the day and then her husband will watch them when she works at night."

"Sounds like a good partnership." Lisa sometimes

wished that she'd found something part-time when the kids were growing up. Then at least, she'd have more skills to offer. She said as much to Rhett, but he didn't agree.

"When I was growing up, my mother always said that everything happens for a reason. You were fortunate that you were able to stay home with your children, and you enjoyed doing it, right?"

Lisa nodded. As a former teacher, she had enjoyed her time with the kids and was proud that she might have had something to do with them growing up to be good, kind people.

"Besides, if you had done something else, then you might not have wanted to open a bed and breakfast, and we wouldn't have met." He put his hand on hers for a moment. "And I'm very glad that we've met."

"I am too. And you're right. There's no point in regretting what I didn't do."

"No point at all," he agreed. "Are you finished?" he asked.

Lisa had set her knife and fork down. She was full, even though she had a few scallops left.

"I am. Do you like scallops? Why don't you finish these?"

"Don't mind if I do." Rhett popped a scallop in his mouth. And then finished off the others. He closed his eyes for a moment, savoring the sweet taste.

Lisa liked that he enjoyed food as much as she did. When the bartender cleared their plates and asked if they wanted to see a dessert list, they both said yes at the same time.

They ordered coffee and decided to share a piece of cheesecake. Lisa only managed a few bites, but they were delicious. Rhett happily polished off the rest. As she sipped her coffee, she felt content. It had been a lovely evening and as always, she'd enjoyed Rhett's company. He was easy to be with, occasionally funny and always interesting. She'd enjoyed hearing all about the restaurant and was looking forward to going there with her children once it opened.

"So, I hate to ruin what's been an otherwise fantastic night," Rhett began. He suddenly seemed nervous, and Lisa couldn't imagine why. She waited for him to go on.

"You know how I've told you about my ex?"

Lisa nodded. Rhett hadn't said much about her only that they'd been divorced for over five years now and it was fairly amicable. Which she'd been glad to hear at the time.

"Well, Gina and her latest boyfriend recently broke up." He paused and Lisa waited, wondering why this mattered. "When she's ended past relationships she's reached out to me, hoping to rekindle something. And I'm not proud to admit that I've allowed it, more than once."

Lisa's jaw dropped. Was Rhett telling her that he was going to get back together with his ex-wife?

He shook his head though and rushed to reassure her.

"It never lasts. We're always reminded why we ended things. And it's not going to happen this time. I have no interest in going back."

Lisa relaxed a little, but wondered why he was even

bringing it up. He looked decidedly uncomfortable as he tried to explain.

"Thing is, a while back I may have mentioned to her where I'm staying. She emailed just before we left for dinner tonight to let me know that she's coming for a visit. She wants to be here for the opening of the restaurant, to support me."

"And she knows you don't want to start something with her?"

"She knows."

Lisa didn't see what the problem was then. "It's nice of her to want to support you and the new restaurant."

"It would be. Except that it's a bit too close for comfort. She booked the room next to mine."

"What? When is she coming? I don't remember seeing a new reservation."

"She said that she booked it right before she sent me the email. So you probably haven't seen it come through yet. I'm really sorry. I know it's a bit awkward."

"Have you told her about me?" Lisa wondered out loud.

"Yes. I told her that I've met someone that I'm enjoying spending time with. When she emailed saying she was coming, I told her it was you and that I thought she should stay somewhere else."

"Oh, so she'll go elsewhere?" That was a relief.

"No, she refused. She said there are no other acceptable places. But I think once I told her that the woman I was interested in was you, it made her even more curious and determined to stay. She always did like a challenge."

"Oh. Well, I guess we're stuck with her, then, aren't

we." Lisa joked about it but the lovely mood of the night was tarnished.

When they arrived home, Rhett stopped at her door and the butterflies came back briefly as Lisa wondered if he might be considering a good-night kiss. He did look as though the thought had crossed his mind, but after pulling her in for a hug, he simply took a step back.

"I had a wonderful time tonight. I hope to do it again soon and again, I'm very sorry about having to share that news. But I thought you should know."

"I'm glad you did. And it was a lovely night. I'd be happy to go out again too."

"Good night, Lisa." Rhett smiled and gave her a mischievous wink as he turned to go upstairs.

When she let herself inside, she pulled up her laptop and sure enough there was a new email reservation from Gina. She had paid fully in advance and was arriving in two weeks, on a Sunday and staying for just over a week, through Daffodil weekend. Lisa had a sinking feeling that this woman was going to be trouble.

CHAPTER 14

As the weeks went by, Abby missed Jeff more and more. She alternated between being strong and fine that he was gone and feeling independent to missing him like crazy. Missing him like crazy was starting to win. Especially as the hormones began to kick in.

And especially after the date night that they'd had the night before. Jeff had shown up to pick her up at 5:30 sharp. It was the earliest that she could ever remember him being home and ready to go to dinner. He'd said that he went in early so he could leave earlier. He'd showered and showed up at her door with a bouquet of flowers.

They went to their favorite Italian restaurant, and she'd had what she always had when she went there—the Eggplant Parmesan. Jeff had the Chicken Parm and a glass of wine while she had a Shirley Temple. It was awkward at first, but after about ten minutes or so, it almost felt like normal. Jeff told her all the crazy stuff that was going on at work, and she almost told him that she was pregnant.

It was a good start. And it gave her a glimpse of how things could be if Jeff took it seriously and if he really was able to change his schedule. He said that he was, and he seemed sincere which gave her hope.

Abby had just finished eating a bowl of tomato soup and a grilled cheese sandwich and was about to slip into her pajamas and curl up and watch the latest episode of The Bachelor, when there was a knock at the door.

It was early only six-thirty, and she wasn't expecting anyone to come by. When she opened the door, she saw that it was Jeff and looked at him in confusion

"Did you try to call me? I don't think I heard the cell phone ring?"

Jeff looked good. He was holding a paper grocery bag and leaning against the side of the door. "I wasn't planning on coming by. I just ran out to the store to get milk, and I got a gallon of our favorite ice cream. I was heading home and had to drive right by here and just thought maybe you might want to have a bowl with me?" He smiled at her with that grin that used to melt her heart. She felt her stomach do a little flip, and she really loved that ice cream. Funny enough, she'd been craving it more than usual lately

"Well, since you have it with you, how can I say no to that? Come on in." Jeff went straight to the kitchen, got two bowls out of the cupboard and filled them with several generous scoops of ice cream and then added spoons. They went into the living room and settled in their usual spots on the comfy sofa. And ate their ice cream mostly in silence.

"I had fun last night," Jeff finally said. He looked as though he wanted to say something else but instead took another bite of ice cream.

"It was a great night. I miss doing that. We used to go out like that all the time."

"I know. It's been along time since we did that. We should do it more often."

They fell quiet again as they finished their ice cream. Abby was lost in her memories of how they used to do this often. When they were first married. Before Jeff spent all his time at work. When they finished, Abby jumped up and took the empty bowls into the kitchen and rinsed them out in the sink before putting them in the dishwasher. When she returned to the living room, Jeff was still sitting on the sofa holding the remote and flipping through channels.

"I'm gonna make a cup of tea, would you like one?" Jeff never drank tea but much to her surprise he said that he'd love a cup. She went back to the kitchen, made the tea and then brought it back into the living room.

"Anything you feel like watching?" He asked she handed him a steaming cup of tea.

She smiled mischievously. "Well I was about to watch The Bachelor. I taped it last last night while we were out."

She knew that he hated that show.

"The Bachelor. Sure that's fine." He clicked over to the DVR, found the taped episode and clicked play. And for the next hour they watched twenty-five women competing for the Bachelor's heart and a chance to get married

Abby had always loved the show and the fantasy of finding your perfect soulmate in just a few dates and then getting married and having everything work out perfectly. Jeff thought it was ridiculous. Abby didn't disagree with that, but she still enjoyed it.

When the show ended, Jeff smiled and shook his head. "I can't believe you still love that show so much."

"What can I say? I'm addicted. I'm always hopeful that they'll find true love. I'm not sure it really exists though."

Jeff frowned. "That's cynical, for you." He took her hand and looked intently in her eyes. "I thought that what we had was true love. I still do."

Abby felt tears build and threaten to spill over. "I thought that we did too. Do you think that we can get back there again?"

"I do. I really think so. Let's put this behind us. Let me move back in and I'll prove it to you."

Abby hesitated, but she really did want Jeff to move back in. She missed him, and she was hopeful that they could make things work. She knew that the only way that she would know for sure would be to let him try. To see if he could keep to the new schedule. If he could then she would tell him about the baby. If he couldn't, well she'd cross that bridge if she had to. She just didn't want him to change because of the baby. Because then she wouldn't trust that it was real.

"OK you can move back in. But things really need to

be different and not just for a week or two—it needs to be a permanent change. Can you commit to that?"

Jeff took her hand again and squeezed it. "Of course. I'll go get my things and be back within the hour."

When he left, Abby went back to the sofa and pulled her softest fleece throw around her. She felt a mix of emotions, nervousness that she'd made the right decision and happiness that Jeff was coming home.

KATE WAS ENJOYING LIVING AT PAIGE'S HOUSE EVEN more than she'd expected to. She felt very at home there and had settled in quickly. Each morning, her routine was the same. She woke up, made coffee and went straight into the office, where she turned on her favorite Norah Jones station on Pandora, and opened her manuscript. She read over what she'd written the day before, making little tweaks here and there. It helped her to get her head back into the story. And then she'd dive in and write for several hours before taking a break.

She usually went for a walk around the neighborhood at some point, for a half hour or so, to get some exercise in and stretch her muscles. She also found that the walking and listening to music helped her mind to relax and shake loose at least one or two new ideas. So that when she returned to the house, she was ready to write her next scene.

She was almost half-way through her story and was excited to send it off to Philippe when she finished. It felt like it was coming along pretty well, at least she hoped that it was. She planned to have Kristen read it before she sent it to Philippe, to make sure it wasn't awful. She knew that Kristen would tell her the truth. She knew it probably wasn't that bad, but she was always nervous that whatever she wrote might not be as good as it seemed while she was writing it.

When Sunday afternoon rolled around, she wrote until two, then went for her walk before heading to her mother's house for Sunday dinner. Everyone was meeting there around four to catch up on the week and enjoy their mother's famous pot roast. Kate was looking forward to it.

She went along her usual route and was almost back at her house when Jack Trattel ran by. He waved, then stopped in his driveway and started to stretch.

"Did you have a good run?" she asked as she slowed to a stop.

"Not too bad. It's finally starting to warm up a bit, and the sun was shining. How was your walk?"

"Good. I think I worked out who the murderer might be."

Jack looked confused for a moment, then laughed as he realized what she was talking about.

"Sounds like the book is going well?"

"It is coming along. I just passed the half-way point today. Living here seems to help. It's so quiet, and peaceful." Half of the houses on the street were only occupied in the summer and the residents were older, so it was a quiet area.

Jack stopped stretching and stood tall. "Oh, I need to thank you. I appreciate that you put a good word in with

Rhett Byrne. If his restaurant does well, that could be a nice account for us."

Kate smiled. "We just told him where we buy our seafood. And then he had a taste of your lobster. My mother put it in her quiche. That sealed the deal."

He laughed. "Well, that's something I haven't tried. It sounds great."

"My mother gave me the recipe. I should make it one of these days."

"Tell you what, I'll give you the lobster, if you promise to make it and share?"

"That's an offer I can't refuse."

"Great, I'll stop by one day this week on my way home from work with a bag of shucked lobster for you. Enjoy the rest of your day."

Kate watched him walk toward his house as she continued on. She couldn't help noticing that he was in really good shape, with muscular legs, lean stomach. She'd never really looked at Jack that way. He'd never been on her radar as she'd moved off-island as soon as she graduated from college, and she hadn't kept up with people that had decided to stay on Nantucket. All of her close friends had moved off-island too. She reminded herself that she didn't know how long she'd be able to stay there either. So, it was probably best not to get too close to anyone anytime soon.

"YOU AND JEFF ARE BACK TOGETHER? THAT'S marvelous." Lisa was thrilled for her youngest daughter.

Abby was finally smiling again as she told them the good news. Kristen, Kate and Abby were all sitting around the kitchen island. Chase had plans with friends so wouldn't be joining them for Sunday dinner. The pot roast was simmering away on the stove. It was ready to eat anytime, but Lisa was in no rush. She'd put out some cheese and crackers and a bowl of peel and eat shrimp, and Kate had poured wine for everyone except Abby who made herself a Shirley Temple.

Kristen nibbled on a shrimp while Kate sipped her chardonnay. Abby spread Lisa's homemade cheddar spread onto a cracker as she continued to tell them about Jeff.

"So, that was exactly a week ago. I wanted to see how things went before I told you all."

"That means things are going well?" Kate asked. Lisa turned the heat down on the pot roast and joined the others around the island. She reached for a piece of cheese as she waited for Abby to reply.

"So far, so good. I'm optimistic. He's been home early every day. We went out to dinner last night, and we haven't run out of ice cream since he's been back."

"That's important," Kristen laughed.

"Will you tell him about the baby soon?" Lisa asked. It bothered her that Abby was keeping such a big secret.

Abby hesitated. "I will. When the time is right."

"Don't wait too long. It would be awful if he heard about it from someone else," Kate warned.

But Abby shrugged it off. "I've only told you all, so I don't see how that's possible. I will tell him soon though." She stuffed another piece of cheese in her mouth and changed the subject. "How are things going with you and Rhett? Has his ex-wife checked in yet?"

Lisa had told the girls about her upcoming guest and they were all equally appalled and curious about her.

"Not yet. She's due any time though. She missed the early boat and texted that she'd be checking in late afternoon." She paused for a sip of wine. "Things with Rhett seem to be going fine. We're enjoying each other's company." She couldn't help smiling as she said it because they'd seen quite a bit of each other since their first night out.

Rhett had taken her out a few more times, and she'd had him over for dinner several times as well, and they shared breakfast together most mornings. She wasn't sure where it was going, but she was happy with taking things slow and getting to know him.

"That might be her now," Kate said. Lisa followed her gaze out the window and saw a taxi at the end of the driveway. A few minutes later, there were two loud knocks at the door. Lisa took a deep breath and went to let her in. She wasn't sure how she'd pictured Gina as Rhett had never described her, but she was still surprised by the woman standing before her.

The overall look of most people on Nantucket was laid back, conservative, even preppy. Gina was none of those things. She had big hair—it fell to her shoulders with all kinds of wild curls and layers going on. It was dark brown and there wasn't a single gray hair in evidence anywhere. Either she was lucky or used a very good colorist.

Her eyes were heavily made up with smoky eyeliner, shadow and possibly fake lashes. And she was dripping in diamonds. She had huge diamond studs in both ears and an even larger one around her neck just above her impressive cleavage. She was wearing a red cashmere sweater that was snug around her ample bust. Skinny dark jeans and black patent leather high heels completed her outfit. Gina wasn't overweight but she wasn't thin either, which Lisa was relieved to see. Not that it really mattered though. Rhett had said he wasn't interested in getting back with his ex, and Lisa believed him.

"You must be Lisa," Gina said with a smile. She glanced around the room and to the girls watching closely in the kitchen.

"I am. And these are my daughters, Kate, Kristen and Abby. Let me get your key and show you to your room." Lisa quickly grabbed the key and led the way upstairs to the room that was the furthest from Rhett's. She unlocked the door and gave Gina her usual welcome speech, explaining when breakfast was and where to find extra towels if she needed them.

Gina looked around the room and nodded. "This is nicer than I expected."

"Thanks." Lisa felt both complimented and slightly insulted at the same time.

"I think you know my ex, Rhett Byrne?" Gina said.

"Of course. He's staying here as well," Lisa said. She was surprised that Gina brought it up.

"Right. We're still on very good terms. We're going out for a nice dinner tonight to catch up. Any suggestions on where to go? I figured you'd know." Gina smiled sweetly while Lisa was taken aback. But she didn't want to show it.

"There are so many good options. I'd suggest the Club Car, it's always good."

"Fantastic. See you at breakfast, or maybe I won't, if we're out too late. You know how it is." She chuckled as Lisa backed out of the room, eager to get away from the woman.

"Well, have a good night, and let me know if you need anything."

"I'll be sure to do that."

LISA HAD A LOVELY VISIT WITH THE GIRLS. THEY stayed for several hours, lingering over coffee and dessert. Even Kristen who usually passed on anything sweet, had tried a big scoop of the decadent trifle. It was simple to make, just layers of brownies, drizzled with Kahlua and chocolate sauce and layered with homemade whipped cream, crushed toffee bits and sliced sweet strawberries.

Later that evening when the girls were gone, and she was in her comfiest pajamas, Lisa had a second small bowl. She glanced at the clock now and then, wondering how late Rhett and Gina would stay out. She and the girls had heard them leave earlier. Gina's loud laughter as they walked out the door had Kate raising her eyebrows as if to say, "Oh, please."

She heard them come home a little before ten, which meant that Gina didn't get her way about staying out late. She smiled with satisfaction as she took her last bite of the trifle.

SHE WAS SURPRISED THE NEXT MORNING WHEN GINA didn't join them for breakfast. Rhett was on his second cup of coffee and helping himself to a wedge of the asparagus and tomato frittata that Lisa made when she finally mentioned the other woman.

"Do you think Gina will make it down for breakfast?" They were the only two guests until Friday when she was booked solid all weekend.

Rhett laughed. "Gina doesn't really get up much before ten."

"Oh, she gave me the impression that she'd be down for breakfast."

He shook his head. "I'll be shocked if she makes it down once while she's here."

"Did you have a nice dinner last night?" Lisa asked.

Rhett met her gaze and sighed. "I didn't have much choice about that. She insisted and said it would be rude not to take her out at least once while she was here. So I did."

Lisa smiled. "She warned me that it might be a late night."

"Did she?" He shook his head. "She tried. I'll give her that. She talked me into one after-dinner drink. But I said no to Brazilian night dancing."

Lisa almost spit out her coffee as she laughed. Many of the island workers were from Brazil or Jamaica and one of the local pubs played Brazilian music on Sunday nights.

"That would be something to see," she said.

He laughed. "That it would." He reached out and took Lisa's hand. "I wished that you were with me last night. Let's do something tonight."

"Why don't you come to dinner? I have leftover pot roast and a dessert I think you might like. The girls loved it." She'd discovered that Rhett had quite a sweet tooth.

"How can I say no to that?"

CHAPTER 15

Kate worked late on Tuesday. The writing was going so well that she lost track of time completely and the hours slipped away. She vaguely noticed that the sun wasn't shining as brightly as it had been earlier in the day. But then she figured out what poison the killer used. It needed to be something that would go undetected, yet slowly make the victim sicker overtime. A bit of anti-freeze slipped into orange juice did the trick.

She was so deep into the scene that she almost didn't hear the knocking on the door until it got louder. Reluctant to tear herself away from her story world, she slowly got up, went into the kitchen and smiled when she saw who it was. She opened the door, and Jack walked in holding a big paper bag from Trattel's Seafood. He handed it to her.

"Your lobster. A pound and a half. I shucked it myself."

Kate had completely forgotten about the lobster. She hadn't thought he was serious.

"Wow. Thank you. You didn't have to do that."

He grinned. "I have an ulterior motive. That quiche sounded good."

She thought for a moment, taking a mental inventory of what she had on hand. Everything but cream. She'd have to run to the store for that.

"What time do you go to work in the morning? Or if you want to come by after work, we could have it for dinner?"

"Dinner sounds good to me. I don't want to have to rush off to work."

That sounded better to Kate too. She could run out in the morning and bake it in the afternoon so it would be just made when he came by.

"What time is good for you?" she asked.

"I'm usually home by six and will need to jump in the shower so I don't stink of fish."

Kate laughed. He didn't smell like fish at all, though after working around it all day, she didn't blame him for wanting a shower.

"Why don't you just come by whenever you're ready then. Anytime is fine."

"All right. I'm off to hit the shower now. See you tomorrow."

"Thanks again for the lobster." Kate watched him go and then went to find her mother's recipe. She'd emailed it to her after Kate had raved about the quiche.

KATE STOPPED WORKING THE NEXT AFTERNOON around four and set about making the lobster quiche. First, she made the pie crust and then the custard filling. It really was a simple recipe. She just sauteed a little onion in butter, then added a splash of sherry and the chopped lobster. She let it cool then dumped it all into the pie shell and poured in the mixture of eggs and heavy cream. A sprinkling of grated swiss cheese over the top and it was ready to go into the oven.

About forty-five minutes later, her nose told her the quiche was done. When she checked, it was perfectly golden brown, and she set it on the counter to cool. When they were ready to eat, she would pop it back into the oven to warm up. She showered and made a simple tossed salad to go with the quiche.

She still had about an hour before Jack was due to arrive, so she opened her manuscript up again and dove back into the story. It was going much faster now as she knew where the story was going, and it was almost like a race to get it all down. The hour flew by and before she knew it, there was a knock on the door. She put her laptop away and went to let him in.

When she opened the door, she got a whiff of something nice. Jack had splashed on some aftershave, and it smelled great. He wore a hunter green button-down shirt and jeans, and his hair was still a little damp. He handed her a bottle of chilled chardonnay.

"You didn't have to bring anything! The lobster was more than enough."

"My mother always said it was rude to show up

empty-handed. I'm happy to open it if you feel like a glass?"

"Sure, that'd be great." She handed him a wine opener and two glasses. While he was pouring the wine, she put the quiche in the oven to warm up.

Then she opened a can of roasted salted nuts and poured them into a dish. Jack handed her a glass of wine, and they sat at the island.

"The quiche won't take long to heat up," she said as she reached for a cashew.

"I'm in no hurry. How'd the writing go today?"

"Great actually. Did you know that anti-freeze used to have a sweet taste? They've changed it now so that it's bitter, but my killer had access to an old jug that was stored in a garage. She added a little to the victim's orange juice every morning until he got sick and died of natural causes. No one suspected a thing."

"Should I be worried about that quiche?" Jack laughed. "Is that really true, about anti-freeze?"

"It is. There was a woman they discovered was a black widow—she killed two husbands with anti-freeze and then tried to frame her daughter for it."

"You must have some interesting search histories on your browser."

Kate laughed. "I know. It's funny, I went to a writer's conference with a friend a few years ago, and on the way to the airport we were brainstorming the best way to kill someone for her story. We got some looks from the other people in the shuttle van—until we told them we were writers."

"You should write a mystery about a mystery writer

who is also a murderer. They'd have the perfect cover… they could just say they were researching a book."

"Oh, that's true. That could be fun, actually." Jack seemed really interested in talking about her writing and shared that he was a bit of a mystery lover too.

"Who do you like to read?" she asked.

"There's so many. Dennis Lehane is a favorite. My college roommate went to BC High with him, said he always got an A in English."

"That makes sense. I love his books too. I actually lived in Charlestown, not far from where they filmed Mystic River."

"Did you like living there?"

"I did. It's so close to downtown Boston. I could walk to work or take the water shuttle across the harbor. I lived in the Navy Yard."

"By Old Ironsides?" Jack mentioned the famous landmark. The USS Constitution was the world's oldest commissioned Navy vessel, built in the late 1700s and lovingly maintained. It usually sat in dry dock, but occasionally was sailed around Boston harbor.

"Yes, right down the street. I walked by it most days on my way to the water shuttle."

"That's very cool, taking a boat to work. Do you miss it?"

Kate took a sip of wine and considered the question. "Yes and no. I loved living and working in Boston, but I love it here too, and it's where my family is. I'd love to stay here, if I could. But there's not a lot of demand for writers on Nantucket."

"There's a few famous writers that live here. Maybe

you'll be one of them." Jack's smile almost made her believe it was possible, someday.

"I don't need to be famous, just make enough to support myself. I've picked up some freelance work though, from the magazine I used to work for, so that's helping." Amanda had emailed another assignment the day before, a round-up article on Nantucket's 'top ten' restaurants. That would be a fun one to research. She told Jack about it as she took the quiche out of the oven and cut a big slice for each of them. She brought the plates and the bowl of salad to the island and they dug in.

"If you need any help researching those restaurants, you know, for quality control, I'd be happy to volunteer."

Kate laughed. "I'll keep that in mind." She took a bite of the quiche and sighed. It had turned out as good as her mothers. Creamy, silky custard and big chunks of lobster. Fresh lobster had a sweetness that wasn't found in canned or frozen.

"This is amazing. Best lobster I've ever had, where did you get it?" He grinned as he took another big bite. "Seriously though, the quiche is awesome. Thank you."

When he finished, Kate offered him a second piece which he eagerly accepted. They chatted easily for another hour or so, over a little more wine. Kate learned that they shared quite a few common interests besides their love of mysteries. Jack also appreciated art and had bought one of Kristen's paintings at an art show a few years ago.

"It's a small painting, but I saw it and had to have it. It's classic Nantucket, stormy seas crashing into a lighthouse."

"Kristen loves painting the ocean. Where did you put it?" Kate was curious to see the inside of his house.

"In my home office. It has a nice ocean view, so seemed like an appropriate spot."

"Kristen has an art show this weekend, at the new gallery downtown. And I think she said it's all ocean themed. You should go."

"Maybe I will." He grinned. "Want to go with me? We can check out one of the restaurants on your list before or after."

Kate didn't have any plans set in stone yet. She knew her mother would likely be going with either Rhett or Sue, and Abby had mentioned that Jeff was taking her out to dinner and they might stop by after.

"Sure, why not?"

Jack looked a little more serious as he asked, "Are you still dating Philippe? I don't want to step on any toes. He is a friend."

"We went out once. He's a great guy. We just want different things. I recently ended an engagement. He cheated." She told him about walking in on Dylan and Ellie.

Jack looked furious on her behalf and sympathetic. "Man, that's rough. Cissie never cheated, that I was aware of, but we just stayed together too long. We wanted different things, and it was easier to stay together than to break up. But she started pushing for a huge wedding, and we weren't even engaged. I think she just wanted to get married, not necessarily married to me, if that makes sense."

Kate nodded. It did make sense. Nantucket was a

small island and the pool of available men even smaller. Jack, with his family business and overall good looks, was considered a catch. He'd be a catch anywhere though, and he deserved someone who was madly in love with him.

They chatted a little while longer, but when Kate suddenly yawned, Jack jumped up and took it as his cue to leave.

"Thanks so much for dinner. I'll call you on Saturday, and we can make a plan."

"That sounds good. Oh, take some of this with you. I can't eat all this quiche myself."

"If you insist." Kate packed up most of the leftover quiche, saving one big piece for herself and handed it to Jack.

"See you on Saturday."

CHAPTER 16

Kristen spent most of Wednesday afternoon carefully wrapping the paintings that Andrew had chosen for the show on Saturday. He had called earlier and said he'd be by around four to collect them. She was a little surprised and disappointed that she hadn't heard from him since the first time he'd stopped by and they'd gone for burgers.

She'd enjoyed his company and thought that she'd sensed interest. But she'd also told Andrew about her breakup, and he'd told her he'd be happy to 'hang out' whenever she was up for it. But she hadn't reached out either. It wasn't her way to call up a man she barely knew and invite him out, even as a friend.

She hadn't thought much of it until this past week, as she had been busy and was still trying to get over Sean. He didn't make it easy though. She had several missed messages from him and finally a voice message asking her to please call, that it was important.

Once all her paintings were safely wrapped and

waiting in the living room for Andrew to arrive, Kristen called Sean. She had a half-hour before Andrew was due to arrive, and she didn't imagine the call would take long. She just wanted to make sure she was done and ready before she let herself get distracted. Sean answered on the first ring.

"Kristen?"

"Hi Sean. You called? It sounded important."

"Yeah, I…I appreciate the call back. I miss you. It's been a few weeks now, I'm just hoping that maybe you've missed me too. We can start over. It will be different this time, better." She liked what he was saying, but she knew him by now.

"Does this mean you've filed for divorce? That's great news."

There was a long, heavy silence. "Well, no. Not exactly."

"Not exactly? It's a simple yes or no question, Sean. Are you getting a divorce?"

"It's complicated. We're separated, almost as good as divorced."

"It's a world of difference, Sean. I don't do complicated anymore. Complicated is messy. I like simple. Divorced is simple. Single is too. Simple is good."

"If you could just be patient and trust me."

"I'm all out of patience Sean. And I have to go. Please don't call me again."

"But, Kristen…."

"Bye, Sean." Kristen ended the call and walked into her kitchen. A few weeks ago the conversation would have reduced her to a pile of tears, now she felt sad, but there were no more tears for Sean. She made herself a cup of hot cinnamon tea and breathed in its heady, sweet spice.

As she took her last sip, she heard footsteps outside the door and then a polite knock. Andrew had arrived.

She opened the door and felt her spirits lift when she saw him. His smile was easy and big, reaching his eyes as he saw her.

"It's almost the big day," he said as he stepped inside. "Are you excited?"

"Yes. A little nervous too," she admitted.

"Nothing to be nervous about. I'll be there, and I expect we'll be packing them in. Daffodil weekend gets crazy."

"It does. Are you going to the parade?" There was a vintage car parade in the afternoon, and people planted their blankets along the side of the road to tailgate and watch the cars and people go by.

"Probably not. I'll be in the gallery all afternoon and evening."

"Of course."

"What about you, will you go?"

Kristen shook her head. "Probably not. That's not really my kind of thing. Too crowded."

"How've you been? I thought about calling you a few times, but I didn't want to be a bother. I was hoping you might reach out to me if you wanted to hang out."

"I'm good. I've just been working a lot. And it wouldn't be a bother. If you called."

He grinned. "Good to know." They had an awkward moment of silence until Andrew nodded at the lined up paintings.

"Are these all going?"

"Yes, they're all there and ready for you." She helped him carry the paintings out to the gallery van.

Once they were all safely settled, Andrew turned to leave.

"Do you have plans for Friday night?" he asked.

Of course, it was the one night she did have plans. "I do, I'm going to dinner with my sister and mother. We're going to the opening of the new restaurant near my mother's house."

"Oh, that's opening this weekend? You'll have to let me know how it is. Maybe we'll grab a drink after the show on Saturday. If you're not too tired. I know it can be draining to be 'on'. At least that's what I've heard."

She laughed. "I'm sure that never happens to you. I'd love to have a drink after."

LISA WAS COUNTING THE DAYS UNTIL GINA'S 'VACATION' was over. Every time she turned around it seemed like she was running into the woman. As Rhett had predicted, Gina had yet to make it down for breakfast, but she'd chased Lisa down every day for something, extra towels, bottled water, suggestions on who to call for a taxi or where to go for lunch or dinner. Fortunately, she did have friends staying downtown and had met up with them several times so she wasn't looking to spend all her time with Rhett. Still, she liked to remind Lisa that they were married for over ten years.

Lisa was getting the mail on Thursday when a sleek

silver vintage Jaguar roadster pulled up to the house. Seconds later, Gina came flying out the front door, screaming and waving.

"It's Delilah, my daughter!"

A tall, elegant young woman with her mother's long, wavy dark hair got out of the car and came over to them. Lisa knew that she was Rhett's step-daughter, the one he'd said was going be bringing his car to the island for Daffodil weekend.

Gina introduced them. "Michelle, this is Lisa. She owns the house where Rhett and I have been staying." She said it almost as if they were there together, which irritated Lisa.

"Nice to meet you, Michelle."

"You too." Michelle turned to her mother. "What time are we going out to dinner? I need to shower and change first."

"Not till around seven or so. We're going to go to Rhett's restaurant. Tonight is their opening night, so he has to be there, but he'll be able to join us once the restaurant slows down a bit."

Michelle yawned. "Cool. Maybe I'll have time to lie down for a bit then."

"Go ahead and rest up honey. We're in the room at the end of the hall, upstairs. I left the door ajar."

Michelle grabbed her overnight bag and went inside. Gina seemed to have more to say, so Lisa waited patiently and glanced at her mail. All bills, as usual.

"We're so excited to go and support Rhett's new restaurant. When are you going?"

"Tomorrow night."

Gina nodded. "That makes sense. Tonight is the soft opening when they work out the bugs. It will mostly be family and friends."

"Rhett said he wanted things to be as close to perfect for us. We don't really care when we go, it's all good."

"Right. Well, I'm off to visit with Michelle. Enjoy your day."

As Gina walked off, Lisa shook her head in amusement. Gina seemed determined to try to convince Lisa that she was Rhett's priority. And it didn't matter a bit which night they went to celebrate Rhett's opening. She understood that he wanted to have them wait a day, so they could work the kinks out.

THE FOLLOWING MORNING, SHE WAS SURPRISED TO SEE Gina walk in for breakfast for the first time, along with Michelle. Rhett had just sat down with his first cup of coffee and smiled when he saw them.

"Michelle got you up, I see," he chuckled.

"Not by choice. She's not exactly quiet in the morning." Gina poured herself a cup of coffee and joined them, sitting next to Rhett.

"You're just a grump in the morning," Michelle said with a smile as she put a bagel in the toaster and helped herself to a glass of orange juice.

"How did the opening go?" Lisa asked.

Gina answered before Rhett could say a word. "It was fantastic. I knew it would be. Rhett has the magic touch…when it comes to restaurants. He always did."

"Thanks, Gina." Rhett turned to Lisa. "It went about as well as could be expected. There are always issues the first night, and we had a minor hiccup when the fry station power didn't want to work, so it looked like we weren't going to be able to do any fried food. But Henry James of James electric got us up and running before it got busy."

"That's a relief." Lisa knew that fried seafood would be a popular and expected item on the menu. It was something people always wanted on Nantucket.

"So, if you have a craving for a fried fisherman's platter tonight, we can hook you up." Rhett winked, and she laughed.

"It's been a long time since I ordered one of those. What do you recommend?" She looked at Gina and Michelle. "What did you both have?"

"I had the shrimp and scallop scampi. It was good and lemony," Michelle said.

"I had a stuffed lobster." Gina smiled at Rhett, who missed it entirely as he was glancing at the newspaper as he sipped his coffee. "I knew it would be good because the one at his New York restaurant is to die for. It's a seafood stuffing, scallops, shrimp, crab and Ritz crackers."

Lisa smiled. "The secret ingredient." Many of the restaurants on the Cape and Islands used the buttery cracker crumbs in their stuffing.

Rhett looked up. "We do a lazy lobster casserole. That's nice if you don't want to do any work. The sword-fish is my favorite though. It's an inch and a half thick, lightly dusted with crumbs and broiled in butter."

"It all sounds good to me. Are you staying through the

weekend?" she asked Michelle, who was spreading peanut butter on her bagel.

"No, I'm heading back today, actually. I'm meeting friends in Boston for the weekend, then taking the train back to New York on Sunday."

"Jillian and I are going to try to come in again tonight. We'll sit at the bar." Gina smiled sweetly at Lisa who had to fight the urge to kick her under the table. "The bar is sleek, black and gray granite with black leather stools. In a big semi-circle. Gives it a cozy feel."

Rhett chuckled. "I stole that idea from Keeper's. Adjusted the design after we had dinner at the bar. Mine's about four times the size though."

He looked at Gina. "If you want to sit at the bar, I'd advise you to come early. I won't be able to hold the seats there, and I have no idea what to expect tonight. I'm hoping we will be very busy. We have an encouraging amount of reservations already."

"I'm not worried about it," Gina said blithely. Lisa was annoyed that the woman was going again, two nights in a row. She didn't stay long at breakfast though. She only had coffee and as soon as Michelle was done with her bagel, she wanted to leave and dragged Gina with her.

"She's making me go shopping," Gina complained.

Rhett laughed. "You poor thing. Have fun." He waited until they were gone and then said, "I have plans for us tomorrow afternoon, if you can sneak away for a few hours."

Lisa was intrigued. "I'm free. What are we doing?"

"We're going to be in a parade."

CHAPTER 17

The restaurant already looked busy when Lisa, Sue, Kate and Kristen arrived Friday night around six. The outside of the building looked very Nantucket with its new blue-gray wood shingles, white trim and flower boxes that were spilling over with wildflowers. Lisa smiled at the sight of Rhett's Jaguar parked on the grass out front, with a sign that said to come to the parade on Saturday.

Rhett was by the hostess stand when they walked in and was looking over the reservations book. The restaurant was already three-quarters full and there wasn't a single empty seat at the bar. To Lisa's dismay, Gina and her friend Jillian were already firmly ensconced in their seats. Rhett smiled when he saw them.

"Jamie, my guests of honor are here. I'll show them to the Captain's table." He grabbed a stack of leather-bound menus. "I'm so glad you could all make it. Right this way."

"Captain's table, how fancy." Sue whispered as they

followed Rhett to the table. It was a big, round table that could comfortably seat up to six people and it had a good view of the open kitchen.

Rhett handed them all menus. "Sandy will be right over to tell you the specials and get your drinks order. I'll be back to visit in a bit."

They all settled into their seats and a moment later, a cheerful young waitress with long red hair tied up in a ponytail, a face full of freckles and big blue eyes, came to the table and told them the specials and took their drinks order. They all chose different wines except for Kristen who ordered a vodka and soda with a splash of cranberry juice.

When Sandy delivered their drinks, they put their orders in. Sue got the baked stuffed lobster, and Lisa and the girls all went with one of the specials, grilled sword-fish. Lisa remembered that Rhett had said it was one of his favorites.

A basket of freshly baked rolls arrived a moment later with butter that was whipped with something sweet, maybe honey. It was delicious, and Lisa reached for a second roll as Sandy returned to the table holding a platter of Oysters Rockefeller. She set the steaming appetizer in the middle of the table.

"Compliments of the chef, and Rhett," she said. "Your salads will be along in a few minutes."

"Wasn't that nice of him?" Sue looked impressed as she reached for an oyster. Lisa agree and did the same. It was a thoughtful gesture and appreciated by all of them.

The oysters were cooked perfectly, tender and sweet and topped with a mix of spinach, breadcrumbs, and a creamy cheesy sauce laced with Pernod which gave it a faintly licorice flavor. Lisa had mentioned during one of their evenings out that it was one of her favorite appetizers. She was touched that he remembered. Kate was already on her second one, and even Kristen, her picky eater, seemed to like them.

"I didn't think I'd like oysters Rockefeller, but these are really good," she said happily.

"Are you excited for your show tomorrow night? Your mother and I are planning to stop in," Sue said.

"Oh, good. Thank you. I'm excited but also a bit terrified. Because of the weekend it's probably going be busy and crowded and maybe a little intimidating." Lisa knew that Kristen sometimes felt overwhelmed around big groups of people. She was such an introvert, and Lisa knew that after an event like that, they probably wouldn't see or hear from her for a few days. It was almost like being around so many people drained her and she had to go off and re-charge. Lisa reached over and gave her hand a squeeze.

"You'll do great. Just remember, they're coming to see you, your work."

"But what if no one buys anything? I'll feel terrible for Andrew."

Lisa smiled. Kristen really didn't understand how talented she was.

"Andrew wouldn't have chosen you for such a busy weekend if he didn't think it would go well. He knows what he's doing."

"I suppose. I'm just a little worried about the prices. They're much higher than usual for me. And the one piece he's auctioning off has a minimum bid that is a little shocking."

Lisa was intrigued. "Really? That's exciting. I can't wait to see it. It must be really special."

Kristen relaxed a little. "You always know what to say. I do think that piece is my best work. It kind of poured out of me. I wish they were all like that."

"Kate, are you coming with us? We were thinking of heading over around seven," Lisa said.

"I'll see you there. Jack mentioned that he wanted to go, so we're going together. He's a big fan of Kristen. He bought one of her smaller paintings a few years ago."

"Really? How nice." Kristen looked happy to hear it. And Lisa thought it was interesting news that Jack and Kate were going together.

"How did the quiche turn out?" she asked. Kate had told her how Jack had stopped by with a big bag of lobster. Maybe he was just being neighborly, but Lisa wondered if there could be some mutual interest there. Kate and Jack didn't socialize much in high school, and Kate moved off-island right after college, but they were about the same age. And Jack came from a good family.

"It turned out great. Your recipe is perfect. I couldn't screw it up. Jack loved it. I sent him home with most of the leftovers."

"Good, I'm glad. How's his father doing?" Lisa knew about the heart attack and hoped he was doing better.

"Jack said he's good. He's been home for a few weeks now and is grouchy because no one will let him do anything. He can't go back to work for another month or so and even then, he'll be limited to office work, nothing physical."

A bus boy cleared away their empty salad plates and a few minutes later, Sandy brought out their entrees. Rhett stopped by to check on them, and they all assured him that everything was delicious. Sue's baked stuffed lobster looked decadent, and Lisa's swordfish was cooked perfectly, nice and juicy with steamed asparagus and fluffy whipped potatoes on the side.

"I was hoping to have more time to chat with you ladies, but we're busier than I anticipated. Which is a very good thing. I'll stop back by in a bit."

Lisa watched him go and realized that she was seeing a different side of him. Rhett was a natural extrovert. He was charming and had a way of making everyone feel as though his attention was solely focused on them. She saw him stopping at table after table, chatting and laughing, yet always keeping one eye on the whole room so he didn't miss a thing.

Out of the corner of her eye, she saw Gina wave him over to the bar where she and Jillian were sipping martinis. Jillian had a sleek platinum blonde bob and was laughing at something the older man next to her was saying. Gina smiled wide as Rhett approached and put her hand on his arm and leaned in to whisper something to him. He laughed and chatted with her for a few moments.

"Earth to Mom…" Lisa snapped her attention back to the table and to Kate who was asking her something.

"I'm sorry I missed that, what did you say?"

"I asked about the parade tomorrow. Did you say that you and Rhett are going to it?"

"We're actually in it. Rhett's driving his car. We leave at noon and drive out to Siasconset and then we'll tailgate."

"Oh, how fancy. What are you making?" Kristen asked.

"Rhett said he's taking care of all the food. I thought I'd bring a bottle of champagne."

"That seems appropriate. Get the Veuve," Kate suggested. "You know how over the top some of those tailgates can be."

Lisa chuckled. "Yes, first time I went, we were shocked to see that one group had their own butler pouring drinks."

"What will you wear?" Kristen asked.

"I'm not entirely sure. Rhett said something that looks 1920ish. I have that dress I wore a few years ago that kind of looks like a flapper dress but with long sleeves. Maybe that with a double-long strand of pearls and a cute hat. I think I have one somewhere that could work."

"I have a hat you can borrow, that would be perfect," Sue offered.

"Good, thanks. I'll swing over in the morning to get it. One less thing to worry about."

When they finished eating, they all ordered coffee but passed on dessert. Rhett came back to the table as Lisa took her first sip of steaming coffee. He set a plate with a slice of rich looking chocolate cake in the center of the table, along with four forks.

"I know you think you're too full for dessert. But you

have to try this, at least have a few bites. There's a woman on the island that makes these for us, and they're out of this world. That's homemade chocolate cream filling in there and fresh whipped cream on top."

They all groaned, but eagerly reached for a fork to take a taste. By the time Sandy returned with the leather check holder, there wasn't a crumb left on the plate. Lisa reached for the check and was shocked to see that the folder was empty, except for a handwritten note from Rhett. "Dinner's on me. Thanks for coming in."

"He shouldn't have done that. I expected to pay," Lisa muttered. She'd been planning to pick up the check. It hadn't crossed her mind that Rhett wouldn't give her one.

"That was really nice of him," Kristen said.

"It was. I think we might like him," Kate said with a smile.

"Impressive," Sue agreed.

Lisa left a generous cash tip for Sandy, and they gathered up their bags and to-go boxes with leftovers and made their way toward the door. Lisa wanted to stop and thank Rhett, but he was deep in conversation with an older couple. She managed to catch his eye and mouthed 'thank you.' He winked and waved and then laughed at something the little old lady he was talking with said.

Lisa noticed that Gina and Jillian were still holding court at the bar, surrounded now by older men who were laughing and hanging on their every word. As they walked out, she saw Gina wave Rhett over, and he went and joined the conversation, laughing and smiling with the others.

Sᴜᴇ's ʜᴀᴛ ᴡᴀs ᴛʜᴇ ᴘᴇʀғᴇᴄᴛ ғɪɴᴀʟ ᴛᴏᴜᴄʜ. Lɪsᴀ surveyed her outfit the next day and felt like she'd stepped into the Great Gatsby era. Her long dress was a rich plum shade with a boat neck and it was slimming. She wore long white dinner gloves, strappy heels, long strands of pearls and the charcoal black hat. It was a warm day for April, so she'd be fine without a jacket. The sun was shining, and she'd picked up a bottle of the champagne that Kate had suggested.

Rhett knocked at her door at a quarter to twelve and she caught her breath when she opened the door. He was wearing a top hat and tails, and his shoes were so polished that they glistened.

"You look incredible. Shall we?" He held out his hand, and she took it and followed him outside to where the Jaguar was waiting. The top was down and there was no breeze but still, Lisa had pinned her hat into place so it wouldn't blow away.

She climbed in and fifteen minutes later, they were at the gathering spot and got in line with the other cars. There was a long line of gorgeous old cars, all lovingly maintained. Slowly, they made their way along the parade route and to the final destination in Siasconset or 'Sconset as most people called it. When they reached the last stretch, Lisa marveled at all the people who had shown up to tailgate and make an event of it. They parked in their appointed spot and Rhett got the hamper out of the trunk. He handed Lisa a huge red blanket that she spread on the grass.

He opened the hamper and took out an impressive spread, an array of tasty snacks, cheeses, crusty baguettes, pate, olives, cold cooked shrimp, potato salad, sliced rare roast beef, horseradish sauce and some grapes. Lisa opened the champagne and poured a glass for each of them.

"Just one glass for me. I have to head into work later," Rhett said.

They ate their fill and sipped champagne as they people watched. Once they were done eating, they packed up the food, then took their glasses of champagne and went for a walk, checking out the various tail-gates. Lisa had been to Daffodil weekend tailgates before, but it had been years since she'd been, and they'd definitely gotten more extravagant over the years.

Some people had fancy grills set up, elaborate sushi spreads, and even a butler or two. People's outfits ranged from Great Gatsbyish to Nantucket preppy with bright colors like pink, green, blue, Nantucket red, and pants and dresses covered with whales.

"I wish I could join you at the art show tonight. Please give Kristen my best wishes," Rhett said as they strolled along.

"I will. She's nervous. She doesn't do many events like this, but I think it could be really good for her. She's already building a following and having a show this weekend is incredibly good timing. She got lucky when she ran into Andrew Everly. Literally." She told Rhett the story of Kristen's fender bender that resulted in a new friend and art show.

"Timing is everything. That's really something."

"That was nice of your daughter to drive your car here. Sounds like she and Gina had a good time at the restaurant last night too."

"They did. She's a good kid. It was nice to see her. Gina has been pretty well-behaved too once she realized I was serious about not giving in to a fling with her. I think she may even approve of you."

"What?" Lisa stopped short and looked at Rhett in surprise. "She really said that?"

"She did. She's noticed how close you are to your kids and said that must mean you're a decent person. I assured her that you are."

"Hmm." Lisa was pretty much speechless.

"I think she also picked up on the fact that I talk about you constantly, and I don't have any plans to leave the island anytime soon."

"I did wonder about that. How long you might plan to stay. You do have other restaurants to attend to?"

"I have good management in place. They almost run themselves, and we have weekly online Skype meetings. It seems to work well enough. I'm not in any hurry to leave. I could see myself possibly staying here. I'll reevaluate after the season ends. We're off to a good start now, hopefully it will continue."

It was only April. The season didn't typically end on Nantucket until after labor day, and for many restaurants, October's Columbus day weekend was the final hurrah. And Lisa had seen other restaurants open with a splash and then fizzle out and close after just one season. She didn't think that was likely with Rhett's place as it was clear he knew what he was doing, but the location was a little out of the way, so you never knew. She hoped he'd stick around, but she knew that she couldn't count on it. She'd just have to enjoy the time that they did have and take it one day at a time.

They settled back on their blanket, snacked on some grapes and basked in the warmth of the sun while they continued to people watch. Finally, around two-thirty, Rhett stretched and reluctantly suggested that they should head back.

"I wish I could stay longer, but I need to get into the restaurant early. Tonight being a Saturday, it's possible that we're even busier than we were last night. I think we're ready for it."

"I'm sure you are. Everything seemed to be going smoothly last night."

"It did, for the most part. I'm lucky. It's a good group of people working there." Lisa suspected that he might have something to do with that. He'd been training the team for several weeks so that they'd be ready when the restaurant opened, and he set the tone, with the attention to service and high quality. That kind of enthusiasm was contagious.

CHAPTER 18

J ack came by a little after six to pick up Kate for
the art show. She was wearing slim black dress
pants, and a cream colored, sleeveless silk top that
was loose and flattering. She pulled a black cashmere cardigan over it and slipped on her favorite black
leather flats. Her one splash of color was a silver necklace
with a pretty blue topaz stone. It shimmered and sparkled
in the light. She wore matching blue topaz drop earrings
and blew her hair out long and straight, so it was soft and
shiny.

"You look pretty." Jack smiled as she held the door
open to let him in.

"Thank you. You clean up pretty good too. I'll just
grab my purse." He was wearing that same cologne
again. Kate didn't know what it was, but she knew that
she liked it, a lot. Jack was wearing a deep navy button-
down shirt and tan khakis. He looked great.

Downtown was mobbed, and it took them a while to

find parking, which was always a challenge in Nantucket. If Kate had been in Boston, she might have worn a cute pair of heels, but with the uneven cobblestone streets of Nantucket, heels weren't practical. And flats were so much more comfortable, anyway.

They made their way to the gallery, and it was already looking pretty busy. The official show hours were from six to eight, but the gallery itself opened at noon and Kristen's paintings were available to view all day. Kate saw Kristen as soon as they walked in. She was nodding politely at three older women who were very enthusiastic about whatever they were saying. Kristen looked lovely. Her hair was loose and wavy, and she was wearing a gorgeous flowing dress that was a tangle of bright blues, pinks and greens. She looked exactly like what she was, a creative free-spirit. She smiled when she saw Kate and Jack coming her way.

"I'm so glad you're here," she said as the three ladies ran toward the server holding a tray of mini crab cakes.

"How's it going?" Kate asked.

"It's just starting to get busy now. It was quiet around six when we started. I think people were at dinner. Did you guys eat yet?"

"No, we thought we'd grab a bite after, maybe head to Easy Street for Mexican."

"Oh, that sounds good. I love their nachos."

"Why don't you come with us? Or meet us over there when you finish up. What time can you leave?"

"I'll be here until eight. Andrew mentioned getting a drink after, so I'll see if he wants to head over there."

"Have you seen Mom yet? She and Sue said they are coming."

"Not yet. They should be along soon."

"What kinds of things do people ask you?" Jack asked.

Kristen smiled. "All kinds of things. They're mostly curious about how I got started and what the meanings of the different paintings are."

"Do they all have meanings?" Kate had never thought about that before.

"No. Some do, but mostly they represent how I was feeling at any given time. My mood literally. Stormy seas means I was trying to fight through something, to figure things out."

"That makes sense." Kate understood exactly what she meant. And it was the reason why the two of them got along so well. They both were creative and sensitive, and both liked to avoid conflict in real life and used their art to sort out their feelings. Unlike Abby and Chase who were more direct and outspoken. They got along well now, but when they were kids Abby and Chase used to butt heads all the time and either Kate or Kristen would play the role of peacemaker.

"There's Abby and Jeff," Kate saw them walk in and look around. Their mother walked in right behind them with Sue.

"There are glasses of champagne in the next room," Kristen said.

"I'll go get us a glass. Kristen do you need one?" Jack asked.

"Sure, thanks. I had one earlier, but I took one sip and then set it down and it disappeared.

"There you are!" Their mother, Sue, Abby and Jeff spotted Kristen and came right over.

They all chatted and mingled, walking around sipping champagne and occasionally having one of the bite sized appetizers when they came by. Kate was blown away by Kristen's newest painting.

"I can't believe my sister made this. I don't know how she does it. I can't even do stick people," Kate laughed.

"It's really something," Jack agreed. "I can't draw or paint either. At least you can write. Creating stories is pretty cool."

"Oh, I know! I wasn't fishing for compliments. I'm just in awe. I always knew she was good, but this is crazy good. It's like she hit a new level."

"I agree. And it looks like we're not the only ones. The bidding has picked up."

They walked over to the bidding book that was on a table by Kristen's newest painting. Kate's jaw dropped when she saw how high the bids already were. The most recent bid was over five thousand dollars.

"And it's early still. It will be interesting to see how high it goes," Jack said.

"I'm thrilled for her." They made their way over to where their mother was chatting with Abby and Jeff and Sue was talking to a woman who looked vaguely familiar but Kate couldn't quite place her. Andrew was chatting with Kristen and Kate saw him introduce her to a well dressed older couple. Kristen seemed comfortable now that she was surrounded by people she knew, and everyone was interested in talking to her about her art. Kate was glad to see it.

"Two of my favorite people, Kate and Jack! Kristen is your sister right? Now it makes sense. Andrew called and said we had to come by for tonight's show." Philippe Gaston had arrived. He gave Kate a quick kiss on the cheek and nodded at Jack. "Oh, my friend Sophie is visiting from LA. She's an actress in my new show."

"It's so nice to meet you!" Sophie was stunning. Tall, thin, and blonde with impossibly high cheekbones and pouty lips. She looked like a supermodel.

"It's Sophie's first acting job. She's mostly done modeling," Philippe said. "I have two other friends in town this weekend too. They've never been to Nantucket, can you imagine? Dylan did some work on our show too and his lovely fiancee, Ellie. Guys, this is Kate and Jack. They're Nantucket natives."

Kate felt suddenly lightheaded. She hadn't expected to see Dylan again, certainly not on Nantucket of all places.

"Hi Kate, you look well."

"Hi Kate," Ellie said softly. Kate noticed with horror that one of her hands kept drifting to her slightly swollen stomach. Her eyes met Dylan's, and he looked uncomfortable for a moment then forced a smile. "We're engaged and expecting."

"That's great."

"Is that who I think it is?" Jack whispered softly.

Kate nodded. She wasn't upset, just shocked.

"Kate, do you know Amelia? Abby, this is the woman that runs the yarn shop where Sue and I started taking lessons." Kate tried to focus on what her mother was saying. So that was why the woman looked familiar.

"Abby, you're the one who's pregnant, right? Congratulations."

Kate watched in horror as Abby turned deathly pale and Jeff looked all kinds of confused.

"You're pregnant?" he snapped.

She nodded miserably.

"Is it mine?" His voice was uncomfortably loud and the room suddenly fell silent.

"Of course it is," Abby hissed. "How can you even ask me that?"

Jeff laughed. "You're kidding right? What do you expect me to think when my wife tells everyone except me that she's pregnant? I'm out of here. You can drive home. I'll get an Uber to my brother's."

Jeff stalked off, and Abby ran after him.

"Well, this is turning into quite the night," Jack said. "I think I need a refill on the champagne. Anyone else?'"

While Jack went off for champagne, Philippe pulled Kate aside as Dylan and Ellie wandered into the next room.

"Kate, I'm so sorry. I didn't know or I never would have brought them here."

Kate laughed. "It's fine, really. How could you know? And I'm truly over Dylan, it just took me by surprise."

"Okay, good."

"Sophie seems sweet." Kate wondered how old she was, she looked very young.

"She is a sweetheart and mature for her age. She's been modeling for ten years, started when she was fourteen." Kate couldn't imagine. It was such a different world. Philippe seemed happy though, Sophie too.

"How's the writing going? Will you have anything to send me soon? I'm looking forward to reading when you're done."

"It's going well. I'm near the end now, and it's going so fast. I can barely keep up."

He smiled. "That's my favorite part—when the ideas are flowing so fast and furious. It happens like that at the end for me too. Wish it was that way all the way through. Sometimes it's like pulling teeth, trying to get words to come that won't budge."

Kate laughed. "That's exactly what it's like. I should be done with my first draft sometime next week. I'll go over it again, clean it up and then email it to you. I really appreciate that you're willing to read."

"People helped me when I was starting out. I'm just paying it forward. Plus, I like your writing and am sort of in between projects for a few weeks. So I have time to kill."

Jack returned and handed Kate a new glass of champagne.

"I should go find Sophie and the others. Kate, just email when you're ready."

"I will."

Jack raised his eyebrows as Philippe walked away. "The way tonight has gone so far, do I dare ask what you might be ready for with Philippe?"

Kate laughed and almost spit out the champagne she'd just swallowed.

"He's going to read my manuscript when it's done and ready."

Jack laughed. "Good, that I fully approve of! I ran

into Andrew and he said that he and Kristen will meet us at Easy Street. It's almost eight now. I'm going to go check the bidding."

"Oh, fun. Let me know how crazy high it's getting. I'm going to find my mother and say goodbye."

Kate found her mother and Sue just outside the door trying to calm down a nearly hysterical Abby. She wasn't usually so emotional, but Kate figured the pregnancy hormones and keeping the secret for too long was too much for her.

"Why didn't you tell him sooner?" Kate asked, once Abby had calmed down.

"I should have, I know. I just didn't want to rock the boat. We were getting along so well, and I'd already waited too long. I knew it was going to be an issue that I didn't tell him sooner, so I put it off, which just made it worse."

"You can get past this," their mother assured her.

"I hope so. He's furious now, but I'll go see him tomorrow and talk to him."

"We're going for Mexican, do you want to join us?" Kate thought maybe it would help to get her mind off everything, but Abby shook her head.

"No, thank you. My stomach can't handle Mexican right now. But I do have an unopened carton of mint chocolate chip waiting for me."

Kate went back inside and found Jack who was chatting with Kristen and Andrew. The gallery had emptied out as it was a few minutes past eight.

"We'll head over there and grab a table," Jack said.

"We're maybe ten minutes behind you," Andrew said.

———

WHEN THEY REACHED EASY STREET CANTINA, THERE were plenty of tables open as the dinner rush was over. They were seated at a table for four. Jack ordered a beer and Kate got a frozen raspberry margarita. Their server set down a basket of hot tortilla chips and salsa when she delivered their drinks.

"Is your sister okay?" Jack asked.

"She will be. She and Jeff hit a rough patch, but they'd been working things out. They had a hard time getting pregnant which is probably why he took it even harder."

"And that was Dylan. What did you ever see in that guy, anyway? He's not worthy."

That made Kate smile. And she agreed. "He was charming and fun, and ridiculously handsome. I never really trusted that it would last, to be honest."

"Well, he's an idiot. But you are so much better off. And so am I." Jack took her hand and gave it a reassuring squeeze. Kate felt an initial jolt when Jack touched her, but it also felt right, and sweet. She relaxed as the tension she'd been holding since seeing Dylan ebbed away. They both turned, and Jack pulled his hand away as Kristen and Andrew came through the door and joined them.

"Hey good news. Guess who was the top bidder for Kristen's painting?" Andrew asked.

"Who?" Kate asked.

Andrew grinned. "Jack."

"Really? Cool. I wasn't sure if I'd still be standing." Jack looked happy and surprised. But not as surprised as Kate and Kristen.

"You were the top bidder? Wow." Kate was curious what the final bid was but knew it would be rude to ask.

"I wanted it the minute I saw it. I could picture it in my living room, above my sofa, facing the ocean."

"And all of her other ones sold too. If you have anymore you'd like to give me, I'm sure they'll go quickly," Andrew said.

Kristen looked overwhelmed but in a good way. "Of course. You saw my studio. I can definitely give you more. Do you want to pick them out?"

"You pick. I'll take whatever you want to bring me. Maybe three next week?"

Kristen nodded. "I'll bring them by."

Kristen and Andrew both ordered margaritas on the rocks and they all decided to split an order of smoked spiced chicken nachos and a box of fish tacos.

The food was great, and they talked and laughed over dinner. Kate wasn't sure how Kristen felt about Andrew, but she thought they seemed really comfortable together, and they definitely had a lot in common. And Andrew was unattached, which was a huge improvement over Sean. Kate was so glad that he hadn't decided to drop by the show tonight. They'd had enough drama for one night.

Kristen was yawning by the time they finished eating. Kate guessed that she'd suddenly hit a wall. She knew how much it took out of her to be around that many people and to be 'on'. Kate was feeling tired herself. It was almost ten, and she was full and ready for bed.

They said their goodbyes, and Jack drove them home and walked her to her door.

"I'd invite you in, but I'm afraid I might fall asleep on you," she admitted.

He laughed. "No worries. I'm pretty tired too. But not too tired for a quick goodnight kiss?"

She nodded as he leaned in and lightly touched his lips to hers. The touch woke her as her senses went on high alert and she kissed him back. When he pulled away, they were both smiling.

"Thank you for a memorable night. Let's do it again soon?"

"I'd like that."

ABBY TOSSED AND TURNED ALL NIGHT. THE ICE CREAM hadn't helped as she'd hoped. It only gave her an upset stomach and heartburn, which made it harder to sleep. When she'd run after Jeff, he'd been too mad to listen. She'd tried to talk to him, to explain, but he wasn't having it. She knew he needed to cool down and process what he'd learned. She hoped after sleeping on it, that he'd calm down and be excited.

She called first thing the next morning when she woke up, but his cell phone was off. She left a message, asking him to call her as soon as he got up. But he waited all day until almost four in the afternoon to call. She'd stayed home, skipping her mother's usual Sunday dinner because she didn't want to miss his call, and she wasn't in the mood to be around anyone.

"Where are you?" she asked when he finally called.

"At my brothers. I told you that last night." He was still in a bad mood and wasn't making it easy for her.

"I'm sorry, so sorry. Can I come see you, so I can explain, in person?" She needed to look in his eyes, hold his hands to see him in order to reach him. She didn't want to plead her case on the phone.

"I guess you could come over."

"I'll see you in fifteen minutes."

Abby quickly brushed her teeth and her hair and headed out the door. She made one stop along the way and arrived at Jeff's brother's house exactly fifteen minutes later. A very grumpy and tired looking Jeff opened the door when she rang the bell. He glanced at the bag she was holding.

"What's that?"

"Our ice cream. I picked up a fresh carton. It worked when you came to see me, so I figured it couldn't hurt."

A slight smile came and went as Jeff turned and walked into the kitchen and got two bowls and spoons.

"Ice cream first. We can talk while we eat."

That sounded fine to her. Jeff scooped out two generous servings and put the container in the freezer. They carried their bowls into the living room and sat on opposite ends of the sofa.

"So go ahead. Explain why you didn't tell me about our baby. When did you find out, by the way?"

Abby took a deep breath. He wasn't going to like her answer. "The day I asked you to leave."

"Are you serious? You could have told me then. I never would have had to leave."

Abby tried to explain. "I didn't want you to change because of the baby. I wanted you to do it for me, because we were important enough."

"Okay. So then why not tell me when I moved back in?"

"I wanted to make sure the change was real, that it would last. You've done that before you know. Changed for a few weeks then gone back to the long hours again. I just wanted to wait until I was sure."

"So, you're saying all this time you still haven't been sure?" He sounded frustrated, and she didn't blame him.

"No. The longer I waited, the harder it was to tell you, so I put it off. I wanted to tell you. I would have soon, I swear. I was just waiting for the right moment."

"So, you're not still unsure about us?" Jeff's spoon clanged in his empty bowl as he set it on the coffee table.

"I'm completely sure. And I'm so glad that you know now. Are you excited about the baby?"

"Of course I am. I was just completely shocked. Especially since the IVF didn't work. So I wasn't expecting that we could do it naturally. Did the doctor explain why it happened now?"

"She said that sometimes it just happens when people stop trying and the pressure is off. So, are we okay now? Will you come home?" Abby needed him to come home. She was so relieved that he knew, finally. But she couldn't relax until they were okay again.

"I guess I could come home." He smiled. "Do you know what we're having yet?"

"No, but we can find out in about six weeks. You can come with me then for the ultrasound, if you want to?"

"I want to."

CHAPTER 19

Two months later, Mid-June

JACK LAUGHED AT THE CASH REGISTER SOUND THAT came from Kate's computer. They were heading out to meet Philippe and his newest girlfriend, Angela, another model from L.A. He was in town for the long weekend and for the Nantucket Film Festival. Kate was excited to go for the first time. She'd always been away, either at college or working in Boston and had always wanted to go, but it had never worked out. Philippe had VIP tickets to some of the screenings and parties and was excited to introduce her to some of his Hollywood friends, producers and directors that he worked with.

"How are sales today?" Jack asked as the computer made the 'ka-ching' sound again. It made Kate laugh. It still seemed surreal to her that people were actually buying her book online. She'd uploaded it herself, had a cover made, the book edited and booked ads to market it. She pulled up the software that tracked her daily sales.

Philippe had read the book as he'd promised and had given her several pages of notes on things to fix. It had shaken her at first, and she doubted that the book was good enough and questioned whether she should be writing. But then, she realized what a gift he'd given her—a roadmap on how to make her book better. He'd followed up his email with a phone call where he told her the book was good, really good and just needed some structural tweaks to make it so compelling that readers wouldn't be able to put it down. She slept on his suggestions and then spent the next week making the changes.

He read again and gave it the thumbs up, and then she sent it off to an editor that he recommended. Philippe also advised against trying to publish traditionally and suggested that she do it herself so she could get it out there right away. He also asked if she'd let him show it to a few people he knew just to see if there could be any film or TV interest. He stressed that it was a long shot so that she wouldn't get her hopes up. She agreed and then put it out of her mind as she hadn't even published the book yet.

"Oh, it's still climbing. The ad must be working."

"It's selling more than it did yesterday? That was your highest day ever, right?"

She nodded. She didn't really understand it, but for the past two weeks her book suddenly seemed to sprout wings and had been steadily climbing in ranking and sales each day.

"Maybe it's word of mouth? People telling their friends to read it? It's a good book, so that's not surprising to me." Jack looked proud, and Kate loved him for it. And she realized that she really did love him. She walked over and gave him a long, deep kiss that took him by surprise.

"What was that for? I'll do it again, whatever it was."

"Just for supporting me. For believing in me." She was so comfortable around Jack, and for the first time, she was in a relationship that was easy. She wasn't on edge or worried about how things were going, she was just enjoying each day that they spent together. Which was almost every day at this point. They'd fallen into a routine of having dinner together most nights, either at his house or at hers and going out on the weekends.

Kate looked around the living room and at the gorgeous ocean view out the bay window. "I am going to miss this place. But I am grateful that Paige decided to stay longer than usual in Florida." Paige had met a man in Florida, and they were having so much fun that she wasn't in any hurry to come home, but she'd messaged the day before and said she'd be back before the fourth of July weekend and was bringing her new friend with her.

"Are you still planning to go to Kristen's?" Jack asked.

She nodded. "That's the plan, for now. Her place is small, but she has a spare bedroom I can use."

"What if I have a better suggestion?"

"What's that?"

"Why don't you just move in with me? We're together all the time, anyway. I know it's only been a few months, but it feels right to me. What do you think?"

Kate felt a rush of joy and didn't hesitate.

"It hasn't been long, but I agree. It does feel right. And I like your place much more than Kristen's."

"How about another kiss then to seal the deal." He pulled her to him and kissed her until she was breathless.

"Well, we should probably get going." Kate shut down the computer, grabbed her purse and headed out the door.

Jack drove, and Kate recognized Philippe's Range Rover when they reached the restaurant where the VIP gathering was happening. It was a cocktail hour followed by a screening of an indie film.

Philippe came rushing over to them when they walked in. A shorter guy with a goatee and dark glasses was by his side. Philippe seemed more full of energy than usual. Kate wondered if it was because he was surrounded by so many creative people and producers he'd worked with.

"Kate, Jack, I want you to meet a friend of mine, Kurt Murphy. He's a director. You might know his sister, Kelly Murphy."

"I love her movies!" Kelly was a tiny, blonde dynamo with long blond hair, big blue eyes and a sweet, Southern drawl. She was currently the queen of romantic comedies, and Kate knew she was also a big reader and had an Instagram Book Club where she often recommended books that she'd loved. If Kelly were ever to recommend her book, it would skyrocket it more than any ad ever would. But, she knew that wasn't likely.

"So, I gave Kurt a copy of your book, and he passed it on to his sister."

Kate held her breath.

Kurt held out his hand. "It's a pleasure to meet you. I loved your book."

Kate suddenly felt lightheaded. He liked her book!

"My sister did too. She's wondering if you would consider optioning it?"

"See, isn't this great?" Philippe said.

"Optioning it?" Kate repeated. She wasn't entirely sure what he was asking.

"Yes, she'd like to star in it, with me directing. If that might interest you?"

Kate reached around and grabbed Jack's hand. He squeezed it tight, and she tried to focus.

"I think I would love that."

"Good, I'll have my attorney draw something up, run it by Kelly's attorney, and then we'll email it to you for your attorney to look it over. Sound good?"

"Yes. I need to get an attorney, but it sounds great."

Kurt laughed.

"I have someone I can refer to you. I'll email you his info," Philippe said.

"How about a drink to celebrate?" Kurt said.

"Yes, please. Chardonnay for me.

"I'll have a beer, thanks," Jack said.

"I'll be right back." Kurt went off to find the bar, and Philippe high-fived both of them.

"I can't believe what just happened," Kate said.

Philippe looked excited for her, but also added a word of caution, "Well, it's fantastic, but I still wouldn't get your hopes up too high. There's still a chance it might not happen. Sometimes these projects take a while to get off the ground, and sometimes they never do. But, Kelly and Kurt have a pretty good track record. It's worth celebrating."

CHAPTER 20

"Kate said she has some big news to tell us," Lisa said as she stirred the pot of tomato sauce and meatballs that was simmering on the stove. It was a quarter to four, and all of her children would be arriving soon for Sunday dinner. Rhett was already sitting at the kitchen island sipping a glass of red wine. He took Sundays off, and the restaurant was closed on Mondays so he usually joined them for Sunday dinner.

Lisa was still enjoying his company, and they'd settled into a comfortable relationship. Neither one of them talked about the future, about what would happen when the restaurant closed for the season. Lisa didn't want to think about it. She just hoped for the best and trusted that if it was meant to be, things would work out the way that they should.

"What do you think it is? Something to do with Jack?"

Lisa turned the heat down to low and poured herself a small glass of wine and joined Rhett at the island.

"I'm really not sure. I wouldn't mind if it's about Jack.

I like him. I think they're good together." Lisa had been horrified when Kate had pointed out Dylan and his pregnant young girlfriend at Kristen's art opening. She shuddered at the thought that Kate had almost married him. Better to have her heart broken before marriage than after.

"I like Jack," Rhett agreed. A moment later, he casually said, "I heard from Gina a little while ago. She's engaged again."

Lisa almost spilled her wine. "To who?"

He shrugged. "Some guy she said she used to date. He's older, and they reconnected. She sounds happy."

"I hope it works out for her." Lisa thought about Kristen and how sometimes it wasn't a good thing when people got back together. She'd had her hopes up for Andrew, the nice young man that owned the art gallery. He and Kristen seemed to have so much in common. But after the art show, Sean had called Kristen to let her know he'd filed for divorce finally and that he wanted to see if they could make things work.

Kristen went back to him since she thought it was what she wanted, and since he actually filed for divorce that it was only right that she gave him a chance. She said she was happy, but Lisa wondered. She never brought him to Sunday dinner the way that Abby brought Jeff and Kate almost always brought Jack. But Lisa knew that Sean had a child and often saw him on the weekends. Still, her motherly sense wasn't sure of Sean.

"Are you nervous about tomorrow?" Rhett asked. Her bed and breakfast was on the agenda for the Monday night board of selectmen's meeting, and Lisa was ready for it. She was armed with information and screenshots of her high ratings and repeat bookings from Airbnb.

"Yes and no. I feel a lot more confident than last time, because things are going so well. But, I don't trust Violet and the others."

"I wouldn't worry about them. I think the board was just appeasing them last time. Your business hasn't caused any problems, and there shouldn't be any reason for them to say no."

"I hope you're right."

Lisa heard footsteps and laughter outside the door as Kate and Jack and Kristen walked in, followed a few minutes later by Abby, Jeff, and Chase.

Once everyone was gathered in the kitchen, Lisa asked Kate to spill her big news.

"Rhett and I have been trying to figure out what your news could be, and we have run out of ideas."

Kate laughed. "I still can't quite believe it myself. There are two things, actually. I already updated Kristen that I'm not going to be moving in with her after all."

Lisa's heart skipped a beat. "You're not going back to Boston?" She'd gotten used to having Kate back on the island.

"No. I think I might stay here a while longer." She smiled. "Jack invited me to move in with him."

"Oh, that's marvelous!" Lisa was happy with the news. It hadn't been long, but she liked Jack and thought he was good for Kate.

"And my book is doing pretty well. Between the freelancing and the daily book sales, I think I'll be able to support myself. I haven't wiped out my savings yet."

"That's even better news. I'm so glad your book is doing well. It's very good. Sue thought so too!"

"Thanks, Mom. But the really big news is Jack and I went to the film festival last night and met Kurt Murphy, a friend of Philippe's. He passed my book onto Kurt, and he liked it. He gave it to his sister, Kelly Murphy, the actress, and she loved it."

"Kelly Murphy did? Wow." Kristen was impressed. Lisa was too though she only had a vague idea who Kelly Murphy was.

"Anyway, Kelly loved it and wants to option it so she can star in it, and her brother, Kurt can direct. It still might not actually happen. But it could!"

"A movie? From your book? That's wonderful, honey." Lisa was so proud of Kate. She'd worked really hard on her book and now someone might make a movie of it. It was incredible.

"Kate that's awesome. Congratulations!" Abby said. She looked around the room and nodded at Jeff who looked excited and Lisa suspected that it wasn't about Kate's book.

"We have some news too. We had our ultrasound yesterday, and we found out the sex of the baby." She looked at Jeff again.

"It's a boy!" he said proudly.

Lisa felt overcome with emotion. She took a deep breath. "Well, we have a lot to celebrate tonight. Everyone, help yourself to wine or beer and let's sit down and eat."

THE FOLLOWING EVENING, THE ENTIRE HODGES FAMILY, spouses, significant others and friends all showed up early at the Monday night board of selectmen's meeting and filled the first and second rows. Lisa noticed that the same people who had protested her bed and breakfast last time were all in attendance.

The meeting was called to order at seven sharp and after spending an hour going through old and new business, they finally got to the request for approval of her bed and breakfast.

Tom Barkley, the new chairman looked Lisa's way as he read from his notes.

"Next up is the matter of the Beach Plum Cove Inn, owned by Lisa Hodges. She is seeking approval to be recognized as an official bed and breakfast. This would give her the ability to advertise and be listed on the Nantucket island tourist sites. Mrs. Hodges has provided us an accounting of her bookings and ratings and her repeat bookings. We see no reason not to grant this approval. Are there any objections from the floor?

Lisa groaned as Violet's hand went flying up.

"Yes, go ahead and speak," Tom instructed her.

Violet stood and looked around the packed room. "I have the same objection that I had before. There's just no need for another bed and breakfast. It's a nuisance to the neighborhood."

Tom nodded. "You may sit."

He looked toward the back of the room and addressed the local sheriff. "Pete, have you had any noise complaints or any complaints at all about Mrs. Hodges business?"

"No, sir. Only complaint I heard is that she only has five rooms available and my wife's friend couldn't get one of 'em because she was already booked."

There was a ripple of laughter in the room, and Lisa relaxed a little.

Tom turned around and conferred with the other board members. When he turned back, he was smiling as he looked Lisa's way.

"Congratulations, Mrs. Hodges, the board approves your home as an official bed and breakfast. And with that, we're done. Meeting adjourned."

"So, that's it then?" Lisa said to no one in particular. Rhett put his arm around her shoulder and gave it a squeeze. "It's official. You can put up a big sign and advertise however you like now."

"I can help you get some brochures printed, and we can update the website and run some Facebook ads." Kate sounded excited about all the possibilities.

"Thanks everyone, for coming. I really appreciate your support." Lisa felt her eyes grow damp as she looked around at her family and friends who had all helped her to make the Beach Plum Cove Inn happen. And she had to laugh at the sheriff's comment. His wife had called her directly and asked if there was any way she could squeeze her friend in. As if Lisa could magically conjure up an extra room. Though she wasn't fully booked all the time, the bookings were pretty steady and Chase had floated the idea to possibly build an addition with two more rooms.

Everyone went their separate ways and Lisa and Rhett went home, got two big bowls of ice cream and went out onto the porch to celebrate. It was a beautiful night. They sat side by side on the old swing sofa that Lisa bought when the kids were small. It was soft and comfy and it rocked back and forth. They rocked as they ate their ice cream, and the warm June breezes danced over them. When they finished, Lisa set their bowls on the outside table and snuggled next to Rhett. He wrapped his arm around her and pulled her close.

"You happy?" he asked.

She sighed with contentment. Her life was good.

"Yes, so happy."

He leaned in and touched his lips to hers for a quick, sweet kiss. Then he smiled and gently brushed a wayward strand of hair across her cheek.

"Me too."

I HOPE YOU ENJOYED THE NANTUCKET INN! THE NEXT book in the series will focus more on Kristen and Chase and a mysterious guest that disappears on her way to check in…. If you'd like to receive an email when the next book releases, please visit www.pamelakelley.com and join my mailing list.

Have you read Nashville Dreams yet?

ABOUT THE AUTHOR

Pamela M. Kelley lives in the historic seaside town of Plymouth, MA near Cape Cod and just south of Boston. She has always been a book worm and still reads often and widely, romance, mysteries, thrillers and cook books. She writes contemporary romance and suspense and you'll probably see food featured and possibly a recipe or two. She is owned by a cute little rescue kitty, Bella.